Richard Carpenter's

ROBIN OF SHERWOOD

WOLVES OF WINTER

Richard Carpenter's
Robin of Sherwood
Wolves of Winter
Written by P J Richards

Published in 2024 by
Chinbeard Books

in association with
Oak Tree Books
oaktreebooks.uk

Editors: Joe Sexton & Barnaby Eaton-Jones
Range Consultant: Harriet Whitehouse

Cover art by Robert Hammond
With thanks to Lucy and Dennis Collin

Richard Carpenter's

ROBIN OF SHERWOOD

WOLVES OF WINTER

by

P J Richards

A Chinbeard Books / Oak Tree Books Original

Richard Carpenter's

ROBIN OF SHERWOOD

WOLVES OF WINTER

by

P J Richards

Spiteful Puppet, Oak Tree Books Limited.

PART 1

Sherwood lay beneath an armour of mist that only the loftiest elms pierced through; their branches cast into golden crowns by the rising sun. Thin spirals of woodsmoke marked where scattered villages huddled along the forest borders and, further still, the oppressive outlines of Nottingham Castle faded to nothing, in an illusion of a conquered world restored.

Beneath the trees, the air was still, dimmed by the layer of fog, fragrant with fallen leaves, moss and wet bark. Dew pattered down where birds flocked to strip thickets clean of berries. In hidden glades, boar and deer gathered to feast on the glut of acorns—distracting and luring the animals within bow-range of any poacher desperate enough to risk the brutal penalties.

The brief plenty of this mast-year foretold a bitter winter to come but, for all the hardships it would bring, those who found freedom in the wild would soon be resting beside campfires without having to smother them at any hint of harness and hoof fall. There would be no forays into their refuge by the Sheriff's men when the weather gripped them all—highborn and lowborn—in its fist.

A bleak reassurance that failed to lift the spirits of the four figures making their way along the road.

Marion coughed hard, muffling the sound with her cloak. Tuck exchanged a worried glance with Robin, who had raised his concerns about hearing a faint crackling in her chest when he'd pulled her close the day before. She had dismissed it as a passing affliction, brewed herself an infusion of horehound and honey and declared herself better. But the fever that struck in the night and had her sweeping the autumn brightness of her hair away from her neck to cool herself while the rest of them huddled in furs, was a warning none of them could ignore.

Tuck had advised Marion to ask for sanctuary at the nearest nunnery, to sleep in comfort and benefit from their medicine. He had couched it as a light-hearted revenge for the herbal concoctions she inflicted on them, and naturally, Marion had resisted the notion with all the spirit and dignity he so loved about her. Soon though, as the bouts of coughing lasted longer and left her weaker, even she was forced to admit the sense of his suggestion— and that, in itself, was a worrying sign.

'The good sisters will have you back with us very soon, little flower.' He leaned in to whisper the reassurance, then saw how the determination on her face was a mask, and behind it was a frown of tight-lipped endurance. Marion nodded without looking at him. His smile fell and, with the smallest motion, he crossed himself. When she reached for his hand and squeezed it, he couldn't tell if it was as thanks or to stop him. They walked on without speaking, picking their way over frosted cartwheel ruts and churned mud. He offered his arm to steady her whenever she slipped, but she kept pace with him. Robin and Much followed close behind, anxious and watchful.

With a glance heavenwards, Tuck silently entreated the Father, Son and all the Saints to aid her; always his first resort. But, hearing the distant lowing of a stag, he called on the spirit of Herne as well, knowing that they lived within his realm and arcane protection. Reminding himself—as he did every day in his own prayers that teetered between the worlds—that heathen did not mean godless.

Blessedly soon, the trees thinned, and the road began to rise towards open ground. The nunnery's perimeter walls appeared though the fog as if manifested by their hopes; a high, stone border that, for all its frugality and strictures, promised a gentler life than the one they had to bear.

Robin stepped up beside Marion, ready to take her other arm and help her to the gates, though he had to fight the urge to sweep her up and hurry back to their forest home.

Tuck shook his head. 'It'll be easier to ask the sisters to take in Marion if she's not accompanied by known outlaws.'

'But they do know *you*, don't they? And they know we're your friends.' Much frowned. 'Why do we have to pretend?'

Tuck raised an eyebrow. 'It's simpler for them to overlook our sins if they're not crowding around their door armed with longbows—I don't want to distract them from their Christian duty.'

Much shrugged, reluctant. 'I'll wait then, nearby, in the trees, until the nuns make her better.'

Marion turned to him and took a breath. 'No, Much. Don't wait for me. Go back with the others.

I don't know how long it might be before I'm well again.' Her tone was candid; she was too weary to soften her words. Her skin was flushed with fever and a lock of hair clung to her damp cheek.

Robin stroked it back behind her ear and kissed her. 'We'll stay here.' Without looking away from her, he held up a hand to reassure Tuck. 'But we *will* keep out of sight.'

Marion was about to protest when another coughing fit took over. As Robin supported her, he signalled an anxious nod towards the nunnery gates; there was no more time to waste.

Tuck hurried up to the entrance. The road was packed hard and worn bare from regular use, and it wouldn't be long before the morning traffic of traders and supplicants would be making their way there. He checked that they were alone and waved Marion to join him. Robin gently led her over, then stopped short to embrace her again. Tuck couldn't hear the words Robin whispered as he held her, but Marion stood a little straighter as if lent vitality by them.

With a sympathetic smile, Tuck took her arm, then gripped the iron ring on the door and knocked it hard against the weathered oak. The sound reverberated through the wood, unnaturally loud in the stilling mist. Accepting it as their cue, Robin and Much—with many backward glances—ran to the margins of the forest.

The sound of quick steps on stone, the muffled chink of keys being sorted through, then a pause before the peephole was slid open. Only the top of the nun's starched white wimple was visible. 'What's your business?'

Tuck stepped closer to speak into the hatch. 'A blessed morning to you, sister. I have brought someone who's in dire need of your mercy.'

'Dire?' The linen headwrap tilted back and bright eyes, nestled in crow's-feet, squinted dubiously at him through the grille. 'They all say *dire*.' There was a rattle of bolts and an almost inaudible mutter: 'Dire need of a wash and a nit-comb, more likely.' The lock turned and the small wicket door set within the panels and ironwork opened as far as a short chain allowed. 'Oh.' She noted his robe and tonsure but didn't acknowledge his status, determined to be unmoved by his petition. 'Where are they, then?'

Tuck carefully moved Marion in line with the gap in the door. He was sure he heard a sharp intake of breath when the nun caught sight of her obvious suffering, but the sister's face remained impassive. The chain was unhitched, and the wicket pushed wide. 'Come inside, my child.' Tuck made to step forward with her, but the nun held up her hand. 'No further, thank you, friar. I will take charge of her. You may return to your… *calling*.'

Marion stumbled on the threshold, but the nun caught her, and despite being short of stature and long in years, she easily assisted the younger woman through the doorway.

Before Tuck could speak, the wicket was closed in his face. The lock turned and the chain swung and scraped against the oak panels. Marion started to cough, harsh and jarring, and several different women's voices spoke in anxious tones. After a moment, an inner door slammed and then there was silence, broken only by the cawing of rooks overhead as they flew off to glean the fields.

For a while, Tuck remained before the doorway, hands clasped in anxiety and the reflexive need to pray. A distant conversation, and the steady clip of hooves approaching through the fog, brought him out of his reverie. He hitched up the front of his robe and scurried back to the trees.

As he approached, Much rushed out of cover to grab and hasten him into the shadows. 'Is she safe? Will God help her now?'

'Yes.' His answer was directed at Much, but his gaze met Robin's; they shared the same misgivings.

'I'll head back and let the others know what's happening.' He rubbed his hands to warm them. 'And I'll bring you some stew later, before dark.'

Much shook his head. 'It's alright, we'll go hunting so Marion's got a proper meal waiting for her when she's let out. She'll need meat, won't she, Robin? To make her strong?'

'No—we mustn't risk drawing attention to ourselves, so we can't have a fire. Thank you, Tuck. We'll take the stew.'

Tuck's lips pursed. 'Not if you don't think it'll be good enough.'

Robin nudged Much, and he took the hint.

'I like your stews. I do!'

Tuck harrumphed and headed off for the camp, giving them a dismissive wave over his shoulder.

'I like them,' Much added in a whisper, 'when they've got venison in them.'

A slant of late morning sunlight lit the clearing, and Scarlet took full advantage of its warmth, his face turned towards the remnant of summer. He sat on a fallow deerskin with his back to a young oak growing straight as a pillar. The fire crackled, and red-tailed kites circled far above, keening. No other sounds broke the silence between himself and his companions.

Then, they heard faint but unmistakable huffing and laboured footsteps.

'He's alone, then—good or bad, d'you think?'

John shrugged. 'He's not trying to run, so he's not scared. If we needed a warning, Much would've been sent back.'

Nasir nodded. He sat cross-legged in the centre of his cloak spread on the ground, encircled by neatly positioned knives and swords. He took up a whetstone and began sharpening each blade in turn with measured strokes, frowning with concentration.

The trudging grew gradually closer.

'I'll go and meet him, then.' John stated pointedly. There was no response. He grabbed his quarterstaff from where it was propped against a fallen beech and strode off towards the noises.

He would have been more annoyed at their passiveness if he hadn't been feeling the same way. When facing their enemies, they shared a belief that kept them fighting long after their strength should have left them, but illness was a foe they couldn't defeat with skill and righteousness; passion meant nothing. Whatever they did, whoever they prayed to, sickness would take or leave them as it chose.

He spotted Tuck's form between the trees, tracing the hidden path that wound through the thickets leading to their camp, and watched with a half-smile as his friend repeatedly snagged then freed his habit from the brambles. He waited until Tuck glanced up and then waved so he was noticed standing amongst the trees. Tuck, red-faced with exertion, waved back as best he could whilst tugging on the edge of his robes.

As they met up John put an arm around Tuck's heaving shoulders. 'Did they take her in?'

Tuck nodded, catching his breath. 'Robin and Much are waiting for her... hiding, close as they can... I need to take them some food... later.'

John raised his eyebrows. 'Tell you what, you cook it, and I'll take it to them—otherwise they'll end up that hungry waiting for you, it'll drive them to begging!'

'Oh, bless you.' Gratitude overwhelmed any offence Tuck felt. He ripped the hem of his cloak from a blackthorn. 'I don't recall it being so difficult... on the way up.'

'That's because Marion was with you—the forest moves aside for her.' John's tone held no jest this time.

10

The fire was blazing, fed with kindling being split by Will. When John and Tuck came into view, he judged the situation from their demeanour, turned away in frustration and struck the axe into a log. 'Nothing to do but wait, eh?'

He summed up their plight. There was no point in elaborating, and they each worried that speaking about it would tempt fate somehow. Instinct filled the gaps left by certainty, and it was impossible to live so close to the earth and not be aware of the strands that made up its web. Staying quiet, so as not to draw attention, felt the least endangering.

Camp duties took over by default. Water and wood needed fetching, there was bracken to be gathered to layer under bedding, goose feathers to be split and arrows to be fletched, bows and their linen strings to be waxed.

No hunting, though, for there were too many foresters on the game-trails. The castle had become suddenly greedy for deer and boar.

The cooking pot, simmering in the embers, held the remains of yesterday's stew. Tuck went over to it, wiped his hands on a rag and set to work topping it up from their provisions.

Nasir handed him a newly honed knife; Tuck tested it against the skin of his thumb, inclined his head in approval, then began peeling and chopping what was left from a sack of turnips given by the villagers of Wickham a week before. Dried ramson leaves were warming on the stones ringing the firepit, giving off their garlic richness. A wooden bowl of shucked sweet chestnuts, pale and smooth as pearls, were diced and dropped into the pot, then he tapped in salt from a waxed-leather pouch. Tuck huffed as he sat back on his haunches to stir the humble pottage, wishing he still had stale bread to crumble in, but the last of it had been gnawed as a frugal breakfast that morning.

The hungry months were almost upon them. He thanked God for this feast.

In the farthest distance, a wolf howled, a single note drawn out till it faded.

PART 2

The Great Hall in Nottingham Castle hummed with low conversation, punctuated by an occasional bout of laughter, or a growl from one of the hounds that lurked under the long tables, catching scraps and kicks. The aroma of roasted meats, the tang of wine, melted beeswax, and strewn meadowsweet crushed underfoot, was the incense of privilege and plenty.

Daylight slanting through the high windows turned the perpetual smoke-haze into silvery wraiths, twirling in time to the harp music. Below, where candles and firelight dominated, the amber glow leant an infernal cast to the faces of the noblemen seated at the linen-draped table at the head of the hall.

The Sheriff assumed a nonchalant pose, leaning against the high, carved back of his chair, one hand draped on the armrest, the other on the table beside a serving of untouched food. But his jaw was clenched, and the light caught by the garnet ring on his index finger flickered as he tapped an agitated rhythm on the rim of a pewter plate.

Gisburne had been at ease before taking his seat, having executed his responsibilities that morning by delivering the required number of deer carcasses to the kitchens, and having overseen the punishment of a gang of poachers caught in Sherwood. He washed flecks of dried blood from his hands into the bowl of petalled water set before him—to the undisguised disgust of his lord—and piled his own plate high.

The Sheriff leaned close and hissed, 'God's teeth, Gisburne, show some decorum. You've the manners of a Saxon serf.'

'I'm hungry—that's the only thing I have in common with those curs.' Gisburne shrugged feigning confidence, un-remorseful of the anxiety he was causing in the presence of the only man who could unnerve the Sheriff.

A man who shouldn't exist.

The Baron de Belleme sat slightly apart from them at the table in a tangible reminder of his distinction, having taken a chair that gave him the opportunity to eat without obligation to conduct a prosaic conversation. The tacit arrangement suited them—the Baron from disdain, the Sheriff from disquiet, Gisburne from denial.

Belleme neither rejected nor revelled in the discomposure his presence caused. 'I can tell that you are curious as to where I've been this past year.' He sliced a line into the meat on his plate, watching the juices bleed out. 'Suffice to say I have been travelling lost tracks, forgotten ways.' He laid his knife on the table and the blood spread like the lines of a map from its edge. 'I have moved through realms of utter darkness, of grey fogs that sap the soul, following the excruciating light of my lord Azael.'

The Sheriff stared across the busy hall, refusing to be pulled into Belleme's narrative. 'English roads can be hellish this time of year.'

The Baron inclined his head, seemingly attentive. 'Have you ever experienced a strangeness that cannot be explained away?'

'I'm a rational man; if I see things I cannot understand, I take it as an opportunity to educate myself.'

'Well said, well said.' Belleme nodded in approval, then leaned forward to address Gisburne. 'And you?' His gaze was a challenge. 'Have you seen anything that defies *your* learning?'

'I am also a man of reason, my lord!' The implied insult leant him defiance. It was easier to reject the insinuation that he'd allowed ignorance to rule his perceptions, than admit to witnessing someone vanish before his very eyes. So much easier.

The Baron blinked slowly, like a hawk breaking its hunting glare.

Gisburne set upon his plate of food; loosed to quell his appetite.

With every passing minute filled only with eating and resentment, the Baron's control grew.

'More wine, Simon?' With a brusque wave, the Sheriff summoned a serving-girl carrying an ornate jug. But her hands shook as she filled their goblets, spilling drops of red over the white tablecloth. 'You clumsy idiot!'

The girl fled.

'I find her sloppiness less annoying than your over-familiarity, *de Rainault*.' The Baron spoke without glancing in his direction. He picked up his wine and sipped. 'You must accept that my visit is prompted by business, not attachment.'

Gisburne, relieved that the focus of Belleme's condescension had shifted, was careful to mask his smirk with another mouthful of venison, but out of loyalty and to defend his allied status, he chose to deflect the awkwardness. 'My lord Baron, I understand you asked to see my hunting hounds?'

The Sheriff seized on the change of subject as if he had thought of it. 'I shall call for the best of the hunting pack to be brought out for your inspection, after we've eaten.' He stabbed a slice of meat on his knife and held it up. 'We have the finest hounds here in Nottingham—we owe our full larders to those dogs.'

'And your emptied treasury to the wolves in Sherwood?'

The Sheriff gritted his teeth but forced a smile and a flippant tone as he turned to the Baron. 'The wilderness has always been used as a hideaway by criminals. Every rich town attracts scavengers, and Nottingham is no exception.'

'But nowhere else is plagued by felons cloaking themselves in sorcery.'

'Surely you don't give any credence to those tales, my lord Baron?' Gisburne interjected, genuinely astonished. 'A man of your learning and experience?'

'I have learned not to dismiss the hold that magic has over the hearts and minds of the down-trodden—if the peasants lack control over their lives, they will try to gain it with folk tales. If they see Robin-in-the-Hood as their deliverer, embodying a Saxon birthright they have lost, they'll believe anything he says—and belief is a power that can be wielded.'

The Sheriff drained his cup and held it out for it to be refilled. A boy ran forward with the wine jug, steadier than the serving-girl but just as nervous. 'If you're suggesting they're insurgents rather than common poachers and thieves, I can assure you it's mere rumour.' He took another gulp of wine to disguise his tension. 'There is no place within my dominion where revolt is tolerated—and my soldiers are more than willing to uphold the rule of the Church over any superstitious devilry they might come across.'

'Oh, I'm sure they enlighten the peasantry with flaming brands, recite the teachings of Christ from horseback, and deliver God's mercy on the edge of their swords.' The Baron raised his goblet in salute, his expression neutral. 'I commend the piety of your stewardship.'

The Sheriff inclined his head in terse acknowledgement.

Both men knew they needed to move past the stalemate.

'So, Gisburne, regarding your hounds—would there be any you could bear to part with?' The Baron gave a restrained smile. 'I intend to start my own pack.'

Gisburne sat straighter and pushed away his

finished plate, pork bones sliding across the gravied pewter. 'I have no plans to sell. I've been breeding the best and want to keep the bloodlines pure.'

The Sheriff took a deep breath. 'What he *means* to say is that the excellence of the pack dictates a price that may be considerably higher than you're expecting.'

'If the hounds are suitable, price is immaterial.'

Caught up in speculation, the Sheriff's eyes narrowed as he spoke over his shoulder to Gisburne. 'You heard the Baron de Belleme. Fetch the dogs.'

Excited barking announced the dogs' arrival, amplified by the stone walls of the courtyard and entranceways. The shouted commands of the foresters holding them on rope leashes, and the strangled yelps of dogs repeatedly wrenched under control, quietened the hubbub of the hall.

By the time the pack reached the centre of the feast, guests were hurriedly getting to their feet, pulling back benches to make room. Several of the hounds strained towards the tables and swiped the abandoned food in gulps before they were hit away by the handlers' sticks. The hall's regular dogs cowered behind legs and skirts or fled into the shadows.

There was a strange sense of the wild encroaching on a civilised scene, a flexing of a subdued but unvanquished chaos.

The harpist faltered, plucked a string of notes that sounded like he was tiptoeing away, then fell silent.

Gisburne waved the foresters forward, but Belleme was already moving out from the dais to walk closer to the animals, his gaze intense.

The pack was restless and distracted, tangling the ropes, their noses leading them from one novelty to the next.

'I want to see the ones with the darkest coats.'

'Yes, my lord.' The lead forester grabbed the collars of four black dogs and pulled them forwards.

'No, not that one.' Belleme pointed at a hound marked with a white flash running from its muzzle to its chest. As soon as it was hauled back, he focussed his attention on the remaining three, reaching out his hand to them.

'Beware, my lord. They're hunters not house dogs, they will bite!'

Belleme looked at the man with disdain. 'Then I shall tame them.' With a click of his fingers the three hounds stopped panting and fidgeting. He turned his palm downwards and they sat, staring at him.

The rest of the dogs continued to mill about, unaffected. The forester watched with a frown of disbelief, then gave a hurried bow and backed off a few steps as he noticed the Sheriff and Gisburne approaching.

'Are they to your liking, my lord Baron?' Gisburne didn't try to mask the tone of pride in his voice. 'Every one of my hounds has proven itself a match for the fiercest stag or boar—they'll track and bring down any quarry you care to set them on.'

'Any quarry?' Belleme kept his gaze on the three attentive dogs. 'Could they take on a full-grown wolf?'

'Oh, yes, my lord. Every grey pelt you see on the benches and chairs here is from a wolf killed by my pack.'

'Indeed?'

The Baron stood in contemplation, long enough for the Sheriff and Gisburne to exchange quizzical glances, and for the interrupted conversations in the hall to quietly resume.

Belleme beckoned Gisburne close. 'I will have these ones. Name your price.'

PART 3

Marion awoke suddenly, grasping at the wrung cloth that had been draped across her forehead to dampen her fever. Her dreams of running were blending into flashes of consciousness as she became aware of the sound of her name being called. She managed to prop herself up on one elbow and whisper, 'Yes?' But when she blinked her eyes clear, she saw that she was alone in the small room. The limewashed walls of the cell reflected the meagre daylight coming in through the slim arch of the window. The thick panes blurred her constricted view of the outside world to a formless smear of blue and green. She sank back into the sheets: they smelled of lavender, and the promise of healing sleep. The sound of her name was the only clarity in the haze of sickness where there was no sense of time passing. Murmured conversations, questions, hymns, chimes calling the sisters to prayers; nothing impinged on her isolation.

The entirety of her existence was moving shadows, or candlelight shone in her face, hard arms holding her up, quiet words, sips of bitter medicine or salty broth, the welcome wipe of cool linen.

Marion.

A man's voice, strong and steady, deeper than Robin's, older than her Sherwood brothers. Older than the trees.

Movement flickered all around her… and she was in the forest, wrapped in a green velvet robe of spring leaves, the sweet fresh breeze blowing her fever away, lifting her hair, crowning her with drifting blossom.

Golden sunlight shone in her face—the gaze of a god. She half closed her eyes against the shimmer and, through the veil of her lashes, saw a figure framed between the sinewy limbs of the trees. Tall and broad-shouldered, his ragged cloak spreading into roots where it touched the ground, bearing the weight of wide, twelve-tined antlers upon his head as if they were no more than twigs.

She bowed in reverence, and felt the surrounding trees bend with her, and then with a thrill of recognition, became aware that all living things within the realm of the forest were turning towards that light to pay homage. Her heart beat in time with every creature, her blood flowed with the rising sap.

She was a leaf unfurling, a seed floating, a song in the throat of a bird, the stamp of a hoof, the clutch of a talon, the crush of a bone between long teeth… a flower growing within the protection of an ancient hollow oak.

Marion.

A darkness is coming—soon, it will be loosed to run through the forest. You must turn it back before it finds every free heart in Sherwood—act quickly, for the Hunt grows in power as winter approaches.

Then, shadows slipped from their tethers of rocks and branches, like huge, low animals slinking between the trees. The woodland grew dark as storm clouds closed the sky but, all the while, the shape of Herne remained clear and constant, holding the light within his form.

Marion never looked away from him, even as the shades spread and gathered around them both, eating the day, chilling her to shivering. Freezing breaths set her coughing, and she pulled the leaf-robe tight around herself, fighting the downward pull of her weakened body.

Marion!

'Marion!'

She opened her eyes to a blur of faces framed in white, a jumble of cheerful voices, arms under hers, holding her up. The rim of a cup was pressed to her lips and water ran down her chin and neck. She drank; suddenly, insatiably thirsty.

'Her fever's broken at last! Oh, thank the Lord.'

A red stag appeared, high stepping through the bracken along the treeline; an animal of fire, it was burnished to copper by the low sun, the steam of its breath trailing from its nostrils.

Robin watched it halt, then it swung its heavy head towards him. The antlers shone, wet with dew, tangled with ripped strands of ivy where it had thrashed its way through the undergrowth. For a moment, they both remained still, in peaceable acknowledgement, but then—alarmed by something beyond Robin's senses—it stamped its hoof, and in a series of zigzag leaps, vanished into the forest.

Robin looked to where the stag had heard the disturbance. At first there was no sign of danger but, trusting its wisdom, he waited. Soon enough, the breeze brought the faint note of a hunting horn.

'There'll be no deer left if they keep hunting like this!' Much was nervous after two days of waiting for Marion, needing reassurance repeatedly and more often than Robin had the energy to offer.

'Hounding that stag is a game to them.' replied Robin. 'But he's far enough ahead of their hunt to escape. He knows the land well.'

'Like us?'

Robin nodded.

'If they drive away all the deer and boar, what will they chase after then?'

'Anything else that simply tries to live its life in the forest.'

'Us?'

Robin hesitated, mulling over a response, then dropping his melancholy frown he turned to Much with a grin and ruffled his hair. 'I don't think they'd want *your* skin draped on a chair, or your head mounted on their wall!'

Much laughed, relieved at Robin's assurance. 'They might want John's though, with his beard and hair and all his furs—they'd think they'd caught a talking bear!'

'Gisburne would keep him in a cage and show him at fairs, for a penny—two if he pokes him with a stick and gets him to swear!'

Their laughter was cut short by a cacophony of jackdaws taking flight from the nunnery roof, disturbed by a bustle of activity hidden behind its boundary walls. They were too far away to make out anything from the indistinct voices carried to them on the wind, but they had a clear view of the gates as they opened.

Much's face abruptly lit with hope but Robin, tired of false dawns, was only concerned with making sure they were both safe behind the cover of a tree before bothering to check.

They watched two nuns emerge and stand for a while in conversation, one broke off and went back inside, apparently called. There was no indication that it was anything more than the usual comings and goings until a slight figure, moving with measured steps and wrapped in a hooded cloak, was escorted out with much fussing by four of the sisters.

'It *is* Marion this time!' Much turned to Robin, delighted at being right at last.

'Quiet! Wait.'

Although they couldn't see any distinguishing features, the upright bearing and grace, and the gesture of declining any help but clasping the nuns' imploring hands in gratitude and reassurance, was unmistakably her independent, resolute self.

Robin was struck with all the emotion he hadn't allowed himself to feel. He had to swallow back a catch in his throat before he could speak. 'We need to tell her… we're here.'

'I'll do it!' Much cupped his hands to his mouth and fluted a passable imitation of a tawny owl.

Even from a distance and shadowed in the deep hood, Marion's beauty shone like a pale jewel set into copper filigree when her face turned in their direction.

Robin felt her smile.

She backed away from the nuns fussing around her. They reached out, loath to send their patient off into the wilds, but she extricated herself and walked away with as much speed as she could muster. The sisters soon gave up trailing after her, knowing there was nothing they could do or say to make her stay any longer.

When Marion reached them, her determined liveliness failed her and she fell against Robin, who caught and held her tight in his arms with wordless adoration and relief.

Much wiped his tears on his sleeve, grinning broadly, collected up the weapons and blankets and set off ahead of them, back to camp.

PART 4

Bright leaves drifted over the empty forest road, gilding the mud. Wrens sang piercing melodies and blackbirds chittered. A badger, snout ploughing for worms, trundled past oblivious to the proximity of Will, John and Nasir hiding in the willow thickets bordering the ditch, their arrows nocked. The low sun shone from behind, directly into the turn of the track, concealing them in its dazzle and highlighting where they intended to aim.

Their planned hunt for a deer to restock their supplies had been cut short by harrowing cries of pain carried through the forest. After following the sounds, and by providential timing (or the grace of God, as Tuck insisted), they found themselves with the chance to save fellow Saxons from the savage consequences of living off the land.

Coming ever closer were the jangle and clop of horses and the raised, arrogant voices of the captors. There was no indication of discipline or discretion; their guard was down.

Tuck had clambered into the branches of an alder growing just ahead of the bend. It was still green and thickly leaved, so he had cover, height, and a clear view of the stretch of road beyond. He leaned forward and with a series of low hoots, signalled the number of soldiers.

Will's fingers tensed on his bowstring. 'One each—whoever finishes first takes the fourth.'

John winked. 'Or we can get Tuck to fall on the last one?'

'Think of the poor horse!'

Nasir waved them quiet and pointed to the road ahead. 'They are coming.'

They raised their bows and pulled them to half-draw.

Will wiped his forehead on his sleeve. 'Wait till they're all in view—don't give 'em the chance to double-back.'

The noises increased. There was a sickening joviality in the harsh voices, and sounds of stumbling followed by curses and repeated thumps. The first figures to round the corner were three men being driven ahead at spearpoint, roped together in a line, arms tied behind their backs so they couldn't save themselves from tumbling to their knees when they were shoved. All of them had bloodied faces from the falls and beatings, and ripped backs from the spears, but were assuredly on their way to a worse fate in Nottingham.

Two soldiers on horseback appeared. Crossbows hooked on their saddles, spears in their gloved fists jabbing at the villagers' backs.

Will and John levelled their arrowheads with their chosen targets.

Two more soldiers brought up the rear—broken longbows strapped to the sides of their horses, and the carcass of a red deer slung between them— evidence that would be used to justify the impending torture and executions.

'Now!'

Nasir loosed. His target slumped from his horse. His second arrow struck the next soldier in the thigh, and the horse pivoted on its hind legs in panic as the soldier clung on, grappling with his crossbow. Before he could load a quarrel and shoot back, Nasir's third arrow pierced his throat in a gout of blood.

Will and John's arrows hit the leading soldiers at the same time. The men grabbed at the shafts buried in their chests, mouths wide, and toppled to the ground, crimson soaking through the chevron insignia on their surcoats. Their horses whinnied and reared, then bolted back along the road, one mount dragging the lifeless body of its rider tangled in the stirrups.

The prisoners—having crouched and huddled in shock during the attack as arrows flew over their heads and horses trampled around them—straightened up with hesitant, hopeful smiles as Will, John and Nasir emerged from behind the trees and walked towards them, longbows down.

With much rustling and snapping of twigs, Tuck came down from his lookout to join his companions. 'We'll need to stop those horses. Can't have them going home to their stables and giving us away.' He patted the shoulders of the villagers as he passed, in reassurance that the knives being unsheathed were only to cut their bonds. Then he lifted his habit to his knees and stepped gingerly between the prone soldiers, making the sign of the cross over each one.

The deer carcass had been dropped and crushed in the commotion, spoiling most of the meat. 'Scraps to add to the pot, by God's munificence,' Tuck muttered to himself. 'Though I daresay I'll still get the blame if there's not enough to taste over the cabbage.'

Behind him, the last ropes were being cut off the prisoners and cast into the undergrowth. The men stood rubbing the welts left around their wrists, repeatedly thanking their rescuers, and trying to wipe the blood from their bruised and swollen faces.

John raised his hand, gently hushing them. 'It's alright lads. You owe us nothing. We'd do the same for anyone made to suffer for wanting to feed their families. Go after the horses, like Tuck says—keep them, sell them, it doesn't matter—we've got no use for them here in the forest.'

'Make sure you get rid of the soldier that's hanging off the saddle,' Will added. 'Properly—no trace—alright?'

The men nodded.

Nasir began to drag the bodies towards a ditch beside the road. When one of the men started to help, he waved him away, firmly but civilly. 'No, find the horses, return to your homes.'

Will was less courteous. 'Go *on!*' He pointed to the road, waited for them to shuffle off uncertainly, then picked up the legs of the soldier Nasir was moving. Between them, they hefted the body into a bracken-filled trench.

John's advice was kinder. 'Stick to snaring rabbits, lads—at least till the lords and foresters have had their fill and moved on. Venison's not worth dying for.'

The men raised their hands in salute and sombre acceptance, turned, and began retracing the path they had been forced down as condemned poachers, their slates now wiped clean with Norman blood.

It was a while before their voices could be heard in tentative and broken conversation, fading into the distance.

When the track was cleared, Will stood over the deer carcass, prodding it with the toe of his boot, his arms full of weapons stripped from the soldiers. 'Well, I'm not carrying it—it's more bone than meat.'

'Good for broth then?' John shrugged. 'What do you reckon?' He looked at Tuck who was deep in thought, stroking his chin.

'I'll cut off the haunches—*and* carry them, don't fret. The beasts of the forest can have their fill of the rest.'

'Ah, you're Sherwood's Saint Francis.' John smirked. 'The foxes and hawks will follow you everywhere, pleading for a sermon!'

Tuck pursed his lips. 'So be it. After all, I've had more than enough practice in saving the souls of dumb animals.' He bent down to butcher the deer, hiding a smile.

A frown of suspicion crossed John's face.

Nasir shook his head, and Will laughed out loud.

The camp was deserted when Much returned, but he was untroubled, still elated at the reunion with Marion. He set his and Robin's bows down, slipped the quivers off his shoulder, draped the blankets over a branch and looked around. There was no indication of a rushed abandonment of the site; everything was in order. He shouted a few times, just in case they were within earshot, but the only answers were the shrill warning chirrups of startled birds.

Though the fire had been smothered, a thin white ribbon of smoke curled around the cauldron. He pulled his sleeve down over his fingers, lifted the lid, and was grateful to find a small helping of stew remained. It was thick and savoury, and he spooned it straight from the pot.

Satisfied, he laid fresh logs on the fire and riddled the embers with a stick, uncovering the coals to let the air waft them back to life. It would be good to have it blazing to welcome Marion and Robin. And if the others were away fetching supplies from Wickham or—as he hoped—out hunting, any food they brought back would be cooked that much quicker.

His mouth watered at the thought.

The smoke rose in lazy twirls, and he watched in a daydream, listening to the bird song. Abruptly, it hooked to one side, as if caught in a crosswind, tracing a line parallel with the ground. Much couldn't feel the breeze that seemed to have taken it, as the smoke streamed away and dissipated into the trees ringing the glade. He sat up confused, holding his hand into the wisps, but he couldn't detect any movement of the air. Then he noticed that the fire was out—not just died down, but cold and grey as if it had never been lit. A dank, chill fog was rising from the earth. The birds stopped singing and the autumn colours of the woodland drained to the hue of rot. Much scrambled to his feet, frightened by the sudden changes, wanting to call out but not daring.

It's Herne—it has to be—there's a mist sometimes when he comes to speak to Robin to give him a task or tell him there's danger. Is this a warning then? Is that why I'm scared?

There was movement between the trees.

Much peered into the gloom. *Not tall enough, no stag's head—it must be Robin and Marion! Herne must've called him and that's why everything's turned so strange—they're meeting up here, 'cause they'd need to talk, wouldn't they? After all that's happened?*

Darkness prowled the shadows at the edge of the clearing.

Please, please let it be them! 'Robin?' He found his voice, though it was cracked with terror. 'Marion?'

The black shapes halted at the sound.

Glowing red eyes found him.

A scream, long and desperate, echoed through the forest.

Will, John, Nasir and Tuck looked at each other, eyes wide, then dropped everything they carried apart from their longbows and quivers and ran full pelt for the camp.

PART 5

The Sheriff's chambers were warm, fragranced with incense and lit with a profusion of candles in silver sconces. Gemstones gleamed in the jewellery carelessly draped over the rim of a carved and inlaid casket beside his silken bed. The walls were hung with fine tapestries imported from Normandy, offering views of an opulent, sophisticated regime to counter the glimpses of mundane English castle life seen through the room's windows.

A meal was being cleared away by the servants, who scurried with heads down past Gisburne and his favourite hunting hound. The tall, wire-haired, grey creature was having its training tested to the limit by the leftovers being carried level with its nose. When it inevitably made a slobbering grab for the plates, Gisburne swore at the serfs and kicked them through the doorway, slamming it shut behind them.

The Sheriff was not impressed by the display.

'Get that cur away from me, Gisburne, or I'll have it thrown into the nearest wolf-pit and we'll really see if your boasts have any veracity.'

The Sheriff wiped the dog's spittle from the hem of his velvet tunic with a kerchief. As he discarded it in disgust, it fluttered to the floor, and the hound yanked forwards to catch it, snapping at air.

Gisburne saw the Sheriff's hand go to the dagger on his belt, and quickly pulled the animal back by its spiked collar, swiping at its hindquarters until it sat down at his heel.

The Sheriff gave a resigned sigh and took a chair by the fireplace, basking in the welcome heat. 'So, has our esteemed visitant gone?'

'Yes, my lord. He left straight after collecting the chosen dogs.'

'I suppose I should thank you for boring him to the point that he had to leave Nottingham.'

'He instructed me to pass on his deep regrets at leaving in such haste.'

'Indeed? Well, I have no such regrets—it's something of a relief to be spared any more of the baron's *singular* company.' The Sheriff waved his hand above his head. 'The atmosphere is lighter already.'

'My lord. He also said he would return within the week to discuss an arrangement that would benefit you both.'

The Sheriff fixed Gisburne with an interrogative stare. '*Arrangement?* Did he give any indication as to what form that would take?'

'He mentioned clearing Sherwood of wolves. I told him they're not a danger to us since my pack has been loosed upon the forest, but he insisted that he could... how did he put it? *"Deliver the land of its native vermin."*

The Sheriff raised an eyebrow, and the hint of a smile touched his lips. 'In which case, you'd best take this pet of yours to kill a fine fat hart in readiness, to welcome the lord Baron back to the castle with a feast.'

Gisburne was nonplussed at the sudden change of tone but decided to concentrate on the reassuring prospect of another hunt. 'Of course, my lord. Right away.' He waited to be dismissed.

Scowling, the Sheriff brushed down his clothes with agitated flicks of his palms, and then scratched at his neck. 'Gisburne!' He jabbed a finger towards the dog. 'If your filthy cur has brought fleas into my bedchamber, then it will be the first course! Now get *out!*'

Robin and Marion sat on a rock outcrop overlooking the forest. The treetops gilded with the late light, shimmered in the breeze, and flocks of birds like small dark clouds rose then settled back into the canopy. A nearby stag-headed oak, its bare and bleached limbs reaching up through the leaves, was studded with perched crows waiting for the dusk.

They leaned closer, Marion's head resting on Robin's shoulder, his fingers laced through hers where they held hands on the warm stone. The turmoil and fear of the last few days was as distant as the edges of Sherwood, kept at bay by the greenwood fortress. Their completeness together was a quiet, sustaining joy.

Marion coughed—a catch in her throat, nothing more. She smiled at Robin's worried frown. 'It's alright. It's just the cold air.'

'Then let's head back.' He started to help her up. 'The sun will be going down soon, and you need to be wrapped up beside the fire.'

'We should've been back at camp hours ago.'

'They'll understand.' Robin held her and closed his eyes for a second, then took a deep breath to control his emotions and stood back, stroking her shoulders. 'Why are these moments so rare? Don't we deserve more?'

'We chose this path, and wherever it leads, we must follow.' She caressed his face. 'But more time couldn't make what we have any more precious.'

His intensity faded into sadness. 'We're always running.'

She kissed him. 'If you hadn't been hunted, we never would have met.'

They stayed, embraced, for as long as they dared, until they knew the light beneath the canopy would be failing and they'd struggle to find their way.

When, at last, they left their rocky sanctuary, Marion took a copper-red leaf that Robin had tucked into her hair as they had walked there, and let it drop onto the stone as a small connection with their respite of peace.

The wind blew it away.

By the time they were following the hidden track to their camp, twilight had fallen, and they walked carefully from path to winding path, noting the landmarks of rocks and ancient trees that marked the way. Although the glimpses of sky still held the blue of evening, it was almost dark under the trees. The branches closed around them in bowers of deepest green and violet, turning the vast woodland into a twisting cave tunnel. Owls hooted and nightjars whirred; scurries, rustles and distant animal calls wove a world of sound to replace the day.

They spoke in whispers and held hands as they stepped through the bracken.

'Shouldn't we be there by now?' Marion was weary and becoming breathless, trying to push through her fatigue, focussing all her effort on being back in a place where she could rest in safety, amongst trusted friends.

Robin paused to concentrate. 'We're close.' He pointed ahead at a dark, broad archway formed by two entwined trees. 'There's the yew gate.'

'Then why can't we see the glow of the fire?' Marion drew back beside Robin, clasping his arm. The uneasiness she had been suppressing from her disordered and half-remembered dreams surfaced, given a sudden reality by fear.

'Maybe they've moved to another camp?'

'Surely Much would've found out that they'd left, and come back to tell us?'

A creeping dread made Robin draw his sword. The last light filtering down from the canopy turned the blade to the blue of midnight. 'Wait here.' He moved forward in a stoop, expertly blending his footsteps into the background noises of the forest.

Marion moved off the track and into the shadows. Crouching between an oak's buttress roots, she pulled her cloak and hood around her to become shapeless and watched Robin vanish into the gloom.

A feeling of being watched overwhelmed her.

Marion, a darkness is coming! Words came back to her from the tideline of confusing images and emotions left after her fever receded. *Soon, it will be loosed to run through the forest!* Her hiding place felt utterly exposed and she couldn't stay where she was, yet the thought of calling out for help terrified her. Who might hear? What might find her? *Act quickly!* She rose up and ran for the camp, tripping over sticks and tussocks, her breath sucked in short, panicked gasps.

Marion reached the glade, clutching her throat, trying not to cough. She took in the deserted camp, the dimming sky, the wall of trees stretching crooked arms towards her… but no Robin. Frantically, she looked for him amongst the branches' silhouettes, the stacked logs, kit and supplies… yet nothing; no comforting figure, no protection.

The sensation of being watched burned into her back, and she couldn't help but spin around, peering into the featureless shadows. Was that movement? She strained to listen, held her breath—there was nothing there. She turned back to the clearing.

Red eyes, glowing like coals, stared from the treeline.

A wolf? Possible scenarios played in her mind; all were terrible, none made any sense. Wolves were scarce and shy. The only time they showed themselves was in the depths of winter, if hunger drove them to raid middens for bones, or if they were flushed out of their territories by a hunting party. Unless one had lost its natural caution from old age or injury. Desperation could make them dangerous.

Marion pulled her knife and held it out in front of her, though it seemed pitifully inadequate in the unblinking glare. She locked her arm straight to steady the trembling of her fist.

The fiery eyes began to shift from side to side, as if the animal was pacing but not breaking its stare. Calculating its next move.

A mist formed, cutting off the lingering twilight. The eyes were set within a void Marion was unable to read, and appalling thoughts filled the gaps left in her perception. Were the orbs opening wider or was the creature moving closer? She stepped back a pace—and unwittingly cracked a twig under her heel.

For the first time, with a slow malevolence, the red eyes blinked, and then, unmistakably, began to stalk towards her. She raised her free arm and covered her mouth to stifle a sob.

Suddenly she was shoved aside, her dagger knocked from her hand. There was a tumult of rushing bodies and the pounding of boots. Her view was blocked by a barricade of shadows, and she heard arrow shafts drawn across bows, the whip of their release, a pause, then the crack of trees being struck and the rustle of undergrowth.

A yelping shriek. The thrashing of something large fleeing back into the depths of the forest. More arrows followed, but none seemed to find their mark and the commotion swiftly died away.

At the sounds of running coming towards her, she crouched to sweep her hands through the leaves for her knife, but before she could find it, she was roughly lifted to her feet.

'Are you hurt?' Robin's whisper was gruff with urgency. 'You should've stayed back! You shouldn't have followed me!'

Marion, stunned by shock, was momentarily unable to answer. Robin's shape became more defined as the strange mist melted away, and the normal dwindling twilight filtered down. She reassured herself that he was real by touching his chest, his face, and then she threw her arms around him. 'Where did you go? Why did you leave me with that... *thing*?'

'I didn't! We didn't. We were driving it away—it must've circled back around to the camp!'

Will's voice came out of the gloom at the clearing's edge. 'It didn't come back, I *told* you. There's more than one of 'em—I never lost sight of those bloody eyes, not once!'

Tuck trudged up to them, puffing. He took Marion's hand and kissed it. 'Little flower, the night is full of devils, but seeing you well again...' He broke off, took a deep breath. 'Is all I need to know that goodness will prevail.'

She cupped his hand in hers and managed a smile.

The unmistakable outline of John loomed up. Much was sheltered under his arm, and Nasir walked by his side, sheathing his scimitars across his back. 'Marion!' John was distraught. 'We were in the trees, chasing the wolf away from the camp. We thought we'd done it, then we saw it back here—I'm so sorry!'

Much's tone was laden with distress. 'I keep telling you, it's *not* a wolf.'

Marion reached out for Much and hugged him, but his arms stayed limp at his sides. She let him go and he stood back, shaking his head, gaze fixed on the black treeline. She couldn't stop checking it herself.

Nasir stood before Marion and bowed his head in respect 'Salam alaykum, my sister.'

Will joined them. He nodded his welcome, his expression serious, gently cupped a hand over Marion's for a moment, then let go and faced the others, determined to get his point across. 'Don't you lot understand? We should've lost sight of it in the forest, but it never stopped staring—never even blinked. That bastard was backing away from us, using its eyes to lure us away!'

John shook his head. 'No wolf behaves like that. They run and keep running—unless they're cornered or trapped.'

'It wasn't trapped. It isn't a wolf,' Much murmured, folding his arms tight across his body.

Nasir spoke softly, reluctantly. 'The eyes of fire—no torches, no moon—how did they shine?' His words seemed to close in around them, exposing the detail they had failed to notice. He waited, but no one interjected. More quietly still he added, 'In my land, such a spirit, a demon made of flame, is called *jinn*.'

'A demon? I *knew* it!' Much, his face a pale smudge in the darkness, looked from one to the other, urging them to agree. 'Nasir knows! He knows, listen to him!'

Will drew his sword as if he expected the creature to leap from the shadows, beckoned by the revelation. Tuck crossed himself and mouthed a prayer. John appeared to shiver but covered the involuntary reaction by adjusting his jerkin.

'Wait.' Robin held up a steadying hand. 'We all heard it cry out when one of our arrows hit, so it can be wounded—that sounds like an animal to me.' He put an arm around Much's shoulders and kept his tone confident, whilst casting a warning glance at Nasir to say no more. 'But we should move to the winter camp now, where we'll have cliffs at our backs and a good view over the forest.' He pointed to the glade. 'Just take what we need for tonight. We can fetch the rest tomorrow.'

Will, Nasir and John took solace in the simple instruction, and carried it out rapidly. Sheaves of arrows, skins, bedding, a sack of vegetables, the cauldron, a few personal possessions, were gathered under the starlight and hoisted onto their shoulders or tucked under arms.

Much hung back with Marion and Robin. He shifted restlessly from foot to foot. 'We shouldn't ever come back here, not ever.'

Robin sighed. 'This is one of our best camps. It's too good a place to abandon.'

'Not anymore. Not now that demon knows where it is.'

'There's no demon, Much, just a mad wolf that's wounded and dying far off in the forest.'

Much grabbed hold of Marion's arm. 'You saw it—you know it's not a wolf, not with those eyes!' His voice dropped to a whisper, and he made sure he wasn't overheard. 'The fiery din must've followed Nasir from his home!'

Marion, utterly drained by her illness, from the trek to reach the glade, and the horror when she arrived, couldn't muster the energy to reassure him.

She spoke flatly. 'Sick wolves lose their fear of people. Nasir and Will are exaggerating, John

doesn't think there's anything evil here, and Robin?'
She invited him to take over the discourse.

'I chased a wolf—an animal—not any kind of demon. You'll feel better when we're safe in the cave and there's a pot warming on the fire.'

Much shook his head, and stepped back from them, disillusioned by their lack of understanding. 'It'll follow us, wherever we go. We're not safe.'

The others returned holding their belongings, and without any more discussion they set off along familiar paths and winding tracks, by instinct, by the faint light of the clear night and the smudges of glowing green from lichen on fallen logs. At each turn or crossroads, they chose the rising path, taking them up towards the rocky outcrop where Robin and Marion had rested earlier. When Marion tripped and nearly fell—even though Robin was supporting her as they walked arm in arm—John passed his baggage over to Tuck and scooped her up to carry her.

Soon she fell into a sleep so profound that Robin, in step beside them, was compelled to repeatedly touch her lips to make sure she was still breathing.

The night was still, the cold air sharpening to a frost. Blossoming ice crunched under their boots as they traipsed, not speaking, each lost in their own thoughts, but their attention was snagged by every fleeting glimmer and glint in the trees.

Watching for the red eyes.

PART 6

The Baron de Belleme, on a fine black stallion caparisoned in scarlet and gold, rode into Nottingham Castle bailey. The horse was used to being given priority, and it tossed its head and struck its hooves onto the cobbles in a proud strut, knowing it could walk where it wanted, and that obstacles and people would draw back to make way. The Baron, his gaze fixed above the heads of the scurrying guards and servants, kept the reins slack in his gloved hands, coaxing the horse on with subtle touches of his heels against its flanks.

Behind him, a servant held the three huge hunting hounds bought from Gisburne, on fine silver collars and chains that seemed too thin to restrain such powerful animals. They behaved as if there were no distractions at all within the crowded courtyard and slunk in tight formation at the full extent of their leashes.

The Sheriff watched the arrivals from his chamber window. 'Good God, Gisburne, if I'd known you had Cerberus in your kennels, I'd have sent you to petition the King to get me out of this hell-hole.' He smoothed back his hair and straightened his ermine-trimmed damask robes. 'Still, there *is* a self-proclaimed king that might well regret this meeting.'

Gisburne frowned. 'My lord?'

'Go down, welcome the Baron with due respect, then you can escort him up here—no serfs in here whilst we talk. I want discretion.'

'Shall I get the servants to lay a table in here?'

'We'll eat after the meeting, in the hall. Just call for wine, the best.'

'At once, my lord.' He headed to the door.

'Wait.' The Sheriff rubbed his chin pensively. 'And three cups. I want you to stay—as a witness.'

Gisburne raised an eyebrow. 'Witness, my lord?

'Yes. Belleme may be prepared to offer me a favour, but I highly doubt that it'll come without caveats, and God knows what diabolical form they may take. If I don't notice any duplicity, hopefully *you* might.' He hesitated and pursed his lips. 'I need you to concentrate, Gisburne—do you think you can manage that?'

With just a sullen nod, Gisburne left and closed the heavy oak door behind him before he could be called out for his small act of insubordination. A servant heading towards the chamber, carrying a basin of water covered with a linen towel, was startled to a halt at his sudden appearance, and received the brunt of his displaced anger.

'Get out of my way, you fool!'

The servant pressed themselves as flat to the wall as they could, but Gisburne still jogged the bowl as he barged past, sloshing water over the floor. He didn't bother glancing back as he carried on to the stairs. 'You'll be flogged if I see you, or any trace of that water when I return with the Baron de Belleme!' He took the steps two at a time. 'And get the butler to deliver a jug of wine to the Sheriff's chamber— the very best he has!'

Gisburne clattered along the passageway towards the bailey, reached the wide doorway, and composed himself before stepping outside.

The Baron had already dismounted, and his horse was being led away to the stables by a squire. As he walked over, Gisburne affected a welcoming smile which was not reciprocated. The three hounds sat motionless behind the Baron, like an extension of his long black robes. Their leashes had been removed and the servant that had hold of them before was nowhere to be seen.

Belleme swept his hand back to indicate the dogs. 'As you can see, they have responded well to my discipline.'

'Indeed, my lord Baron. A credit to your training and care.' In truth, Gisburne hardly recognised the animals he had sold a few days previously. Their coats shone like polished ebony, their behaviour was as serene as if they had never lived in a noisy, exuberant pack. And their eyes—there was something indefinable. They were not the brown he remembered; they were a shade brighter, larger— more *knowing*. He suppressed a shiver of unease and empathy for the Sheriff's caution.

He took refuge in etiquette. 'My lord Baron, allow me to show you up to the chambers.'

A thin, belated smile. 'Of course. Lead on.'

When they reached the doorway, Gisburne turned to invite the Baron to enter ahead of him but was confronted with an issue he hadn't anticipated. The dogs were following the Baron, who appeared to have every intention of bringing them inside. Having recently aggravated the Sheriff with his own hound, Gisburne was unhappy at the prospect of having to excuse the presence of three more.

The Baron noted his apprehension. 'They will remain silent, and they will not move—unless I command them to.'

Gisburne couldn't help but admire how the reassurance sounded like a threat. He inclined his head and let them through.

Belleme's cloak billowed like a thundercloud as he strode through the corridor, the dogs at his heel. The intimidating aura cleared the way more effectively than any announcement of his arrival and sent members of the household darting into doorways to avoid his approach. Even Gisburne trailed several steps behind, unwilling to be closer.

The hounds moved as one, flanks and hindquarters touching. They were almost in step but for the one in the centre, whose back right leg lagged slightly. The discrepancy caught Gisburne's attention; a hint of vulnerability that was at odds with the menace.

The Sheriff already had the door to his chamber open wide and was waiting just inside, lit with a shaft of light from the window that glittered on his chain of office, the gold threads in his clothing and the gems in his rings. 'Welcome, my lord Belleme. I trust your journey was uneventful?'

'It was, until I encountered wolves in the forest—but my hounds saw them off.'

The Sheriff kept his expression neutral. 'I'm pleased to hear that your new acquisitions have already been useful.'

'Extremely. And they could be for you as well, de Rainault, if you so wish.'

He strode in with the dogs and positioned himself by the window, cutting away the light and casting a long shadow across the room. The Sheriff moved to the fireplace, where a low table bore a jug of wine and jewelled goblets. He settled on one of the elaborately carved chairs draped with furs, that were set facing each other within the orange glow, and invited the Baron to sit. He poured the wine and offered it across, without showing any curiosity about the huge dogs that laid themselves on the floor beside Belleme, fixing their wide stares on the flames.

Gisburne closed the door as softly as possible and stood awkwardly, awaiting an order to join them that never came. Resigning himself to guard duty, he straightened his posture and stood with his back to the oak panels, head high, glowering at nothing.

'So, my lord Baron, I understand that you're proposing a possible solution to an inconvenience

I've been enduring?' The Sheriff took a deep draught but then put the cup down on the table, not wanting to lose his edge.

The Baron inhaled the wine's aroma before drinking and nodded his approval of its quality. 'I have refined the hounds' behaviour and accentuated their abilities—every hunting skill that Sir Guy commended to me has been magnified tenfold.'

'That is impressive, undoubtedly, but why is that relevant to me? I have more than enough game for the castle's needs, and the occasional rogue wolf is easily dealt with by my foresters or Gisburne and his soldiers.'

Belleme finished his wine and placed the goblet down. He steepled his fingers in front of his lips, evaluating a thought. 'We could dance around the subject for a while. You can attempt to save face whilst I finish your excellent wine, but ultimately, we will end up discussing how you can recompense me for ridding you of Robin in the Hood.' He reached beside his chair to stroke the head of the nearest dog, who didn't look away from the fire. 'We are both busy men, de Rainault.'

The Sheriff glanced over at Gisburne to check his attentiveness but was exasperated to see a look of confusion that showed he hadn't managed to deduce the real reason for the meeting, despite the many hints.

He bought thinking time by refilling Belleme's cup. 'I assume your dogs would be central to this plan?'

'I have tested them. They have shown themselves more than capable of outwitting human quarry.' He lifted his gloved hand from the dog's motionless head and leaned back in his chair. 'I am willing to devote the efforts of my hounds to seek out and kill the Wolfsheads infesting Sherwood. What I ask in return is that you allow me to keep Robin in the Hood as my prisoner.'

'Out of the question! I want him dead!' The Sheriff couldn't contain his triggered outrage. 'I need the body of Hood to display from the highest gibbet in Nottingham! No one will believe he's gone otherwise—he'll continue to be a rallying point for every Saxon thief and rebel in the north!'

'Quite the opposite. If I reduce him to a pitiful slave, he ceases to be an inspiration—and when I have him under my control, whatever magical connection he has with the spirits of the land become mine.' He raised his goblet and swirled its contents as if scrying the red liquid. 'If you wish to scatter the acolytes, you must first destroy the priest.'

The Sheriff frowned. 'What? Are you referring to that stinking stag-god he serves?'

'De Rainault.' Belleme gave a weary sigh. 'You have all the information that concerns you—all that I am prepared to divulge. I need Hood but I'm willing to remove his followers as well, for our mutual advantage and to cement our relationship. I swear upon my lord Azael you will not be further obligated to me.' The dog that had been stroked by Belleme deliberately looked over at Gisburne, its stare holding the reflection of the flames. 'So, there is no need to watch out for any subterfuge.'

The Sheriff got up, self-consciously wiping a sheen of sweat from his brow. He stood to one side of the fireplace out of the direct heat and jabbed a finger at Gisburne. 'Go! You're dismissed!'

He left without answering, opening and slamming the door in one swift motion.

The hound settled back to watching the fire. Belleme's brief amusement dropped like a mask. 'If we may speak candidly now?' He exhaled condescension. 'We are men of two different worlds, Robert. Yours is temporal, mine is… how might one say? *Other*. In cooperation, we can achieve far more than alone—our reach in both realms can be extended.'

The Sheriff suddenly missed the touchstone of Gisburne's ignorant detachment, his ordinariness. Everything in the room was altering: the shadows bled into the prone forms of the dogs and on into the folds of Belleme's black robes; the chairs were basalt rocks, the fireplace a molten cave mouth.

He crossed his arms over his chest, jutted his chin and adopted his most commanding stance, bolstering himself with the advantage that the Baron remained seated. 'Let's make this perfectly clear: I want nothing from you. I will give my permission for you to hunt within the forest of Sherwood— what you hunt and why will remain your business, provided it doesn't interfere with the governing of my lands, and that I'm in no way associated with whatever you're planning.' Then, a hint of his fear slipped through the caveats. 'I have no intention of descending into the pit with you.'

Belleme sneered. 'I find it amusing that you believe it's a destination you haven't already chosen.' He drained his cup. 'None of us can escape our ordained path, Robert. Therefore, it's up to us to line the way with power, pleasure and riches.' He rose from his chair, stood tall, radiating refinement and effortless authority. The hounds stretched and got up, waiting for the next signal. Though their coats were glossed by the heat of the fire, none of them were panting. One held up the weight of its back leg, the tips of its claws just touching the floor. A small patch of fur on its hindquarters looked to have been cut, only showing up because of the low, sidelong light.

The Sheriff noticed and seized on the opportunity to divert the dialogue onto something prosaic, even though he felt no sympathy. 'Has your dog been injured? I can call for a servant to bring water and salve, if you wish?'

'No, there's no need. It's just a wound sustained during training and will heal on its own. But thank you for your concern—and thank you for your hospitality, especially the excellent wine.' Belleme strode towards the door, and the dogs and shadows followed. 'I shall exercise your gracious permit to hunt over the next few days. I would further appreciate if your foresters are made to understand that I do not require their services, and that I should be allowed to experience the full seclusion of Sherwood.'

'Of course, my lord Baron.' It was an easy request to fulfil, and one the foresters would surely be relieved to obey. 'Would you like me to post soldiers to prevent villagers from entering whilst you hunt?'

'No, that won't be necessary. They're inconsequential, alive or dead—and it will be a useful test of my hounds' ability to discriminate if they flush out a serf instead of a Wolfshead.'

'Indeed.' Relieved to be back on common ground, the Sheriff opened the door for Belleme, expecting to find Gisburne waiting outside, but the passageway was deserted. He gritted his teeth and forced a smile. 'Excuse me.' He took a breath and bellowed. '*Gisburne!*'

There was a short pause, then the thump of boots coming up the stone stairs.

'Yes, my lord?' Gisburne was reluctant to stand near Belleme and his dogs, and kept one foot on the step below, poised to flinch back, even though he maintained an otherwise soldierly posture.

'Escort the Baron to his horse—give him every assistance and any supplies he requires.'

'Yes, my lord.' He moved back to make way as the Sheriff bade a stilted farewell to his guest. Belleme swept past without acknowledging Gisburne. The three dogs trod the stairs in time with one another, their claws on the stone like the scratched beat of a gallows drum. He waited as long as professional manners would allow before following behind.

The Sheriff watched them out of sight, then went back into his chamber and closed the door. He examined the room from where he stood, unsure of what he was checking for, as he pulled open the neck of his robes and let air cool his throat and chest. The eldritch patches of darkness were gone, the fire had slumped into a heap of golden embers, and the wan afternoon light through the windows calmed the strangeness. He could almost convince himself it was all in his imagination, prompted by the sinister aura that Belleme cultivated, but denial alone wasn't a match for the depths of the disturbance. He went over to a chair and sat with the jug of wine and his goblet clenched in his hands, hunched and staring into nothing, drinking until the pitcher was empty.

PART 7

'What's wrong Robin?' Marion touched the hand he clasped on Albion's hilt. 'What are you looking for?'

Robin blinked as if startled from a dream, then sighed and stretched. 'Nothing.'

'You've been on watch for hours. It's getting dark. Come and sit by the fire and have something to eat.' She held out her hand for him to take, and he accepted the help to stand, aware—now he was moving—that he'd been sitting in the same position on the rock for too long.

He kissed her cheek and kept hold of her hand, but Marion noted how he made no move to sheath the sword. 'You think that wolf will be back, don't you?'

'If there's more than one—like Will says—we need to be careful. They're clever and persistent.'

Marion pulled him to a halt. They were still far enough from their shelter to speak without being overheard. 'That's not why you're worried—it's not why *I'm* worried. There's something else, isn't there? You *do* believe Nasir.'

Robin put the sword away and took her hand, giving a reassuring smile. 'I want you to save all your strength for healing, not worrying about this. We've dealt with wolves before. It's nothing to be scared about—we'll just keep watch and drive them off if they try their luck. They're hungry animals, that's all.'

'In the middle of winter perhaps, after weeks of snow and ice. Not now, in autumn when there's game everywhere.' She frowned at him, holding his gaze. 'Don't try to protect me by lying. Save that for Much. I know—I can *sense*—there's something evil moving through the forest.' She shook her head earnestly, her auburn locks tumbling. 'It's something that's been in my mind since I left the nunnery. I can't explain it. I tried to forget but it's like a shadow over my heart.' Her eyes shone with tears. 'I thought it was the sickness that left me with this dread: the fear of being vulnerable, of death, I suppose… but in the glade, when I saw those red flames staring at me, I knew that feeling was a warning.'

Robin's façade dropped. Seriousness clouded his face, and he spoke in a whisper. 'I want, more than anything, to keep it away from you—from all of us.' He glanced back over the darkening landscape. 'I don't know if I can.'

Marion took a moment to adjust to the admission. Her last, subconscious hope that they were dealing with something within their power was lost.

She took a breath and steadied herself. 'We need to tell the others. Even Much.'

Robin nodded. 'Carefully, though. I'll let him keep Albion for a while. It'll make him feel safer.'

'Should we move from here?'

'No, this is still the best place for our camp. Nothing can stalk us up here without being seen, and the ravens nesting on the ridge will call out a warning if anything comes close.' He squared his shoulders. 'As soon as dawn breaks tomorrow, I'll go to find Herne.'

'But you said he's wandering the deep land, that he's too far away to speak to you until midwinter!'

'I'll go to his sanctuary. I'll call him. I'm his son, he has to answer me.' He forced a tone of determination to give himself confidence in the strategy, and to reassure Marion.

68

Although a dozen alternative plans span in her head, none were any better. She put her arms around him and held firm. 'Bring back the arrow, even if Herne isn't in the caves. We need it here with us.'

'I will.'

A hand, a hoof, a paw… Herne rubbed ochre into the wet rock walls and floor of his cave, where the filaments of roots reaching in from the outside starved and faltered. Moss filled the older patches, layering its own language over his designs. The rhythm of his heartbeat was the ticking of days, of years, of centuries. The cold was creeping over his body and over the land, encasing him in the white of near-death, but the heat in his blood was the buried web that suspended hope out the reach of winter, keeping the sleeping seeds alive.

A hoof, a paw, an arrow… He scooped red mud from a wolf skull palette and marked the point where light from the upper world died. He worked in the shadows cast by a fire he had kindled from tiny, dry bones gathered in the dark. Shapes swayed and settled as he coaxed them from their outlines in the stone.

A paw, an arrow, a flame… The tracing of his fingertips stalled at an unfamiliar seam in the rock face. A vein of black, thin and sharp-edged: a fresh crack formed where a shift of pressure couldn't be borne. He rested his palm over the split and felt the flow of icy air like a long, indrawn breath, tasting his scent, testing his fragility.

An arrow, a flame, a flower… He pressed the skull close to the stone and thumbed the last of the ochre into the crack until it was sealed. From that line he created the stem and leaves of a flower. Out of a fragile hare's skull, he dabbed chalk paste to make the petals, then picked up a dished amber pebble full of yellow ochre and drew a halo around the small bloom, with rays pointing outwards in a circle of protection.

A flame, a flower, the rising sun… Warmed by the memories of every dawn he had witnessed, and all those that had come before, he cradled their light in his earthen-stained arms, holding fast to the faith that it would return.

A flower, the rising sun… the call of a child.

PART 8

An abandoned roadway through Sherwood—once leading to the village of Loxley, now a river of ferns overhung with branches. The measured beat of hooves, a low and nervous whinny. The great trees that bordered the track blotted out the lingering twilight, so that the moving figures were only dimly illuminated by a lantern swaying with the gait of the steed. All was in silhouette or fringed with its sullen glow.

Black horse, black-robed rider. Black dogs.

They came to a halt without any word of command or tug of the reins. The rider dismounted and held the light above the three hounds. The candle guttered as if starved of air, and the weak illumination it cast was lost altogether in their fur, merely outlining their forms against the ground.

With a shake of the lantern, the candle was snuffed in its molten wax, yet a radiance remained around the dogs; a faint, sickly marsh-light that extended from their bodies and made them larger still. Then an incantation hushed the calm nocturnal refrain of the woods. The undergrowth and canopy shivered at the sound as creatures fled and birds roused, none giving any alarm call; instinct compelling them to a swift and silent escape. The chanting was akin to the humming in a throat before a growl, and soon the humanity in the voice was overlaid with a diabolic snarling. The horse—despite its conditioning—backed away trembling and with ears flattened, but the dogs at Belleme's feet crouched, ready to run, panting with eagerness, their eyes shining red, swollen in their sockets, stretching back the skin of their lids.

With a final intonation of long syllables that blended and twisted like snakes, the hackles on the hounds bristled. They raised their heads and howled the last note, then fragmented it into a hideous harmony that gave voice to the decay of the failing year, the cold and the dark, the starvation and misery. The black dogs passed it from one to the other as they took a breath, so that it spread in waves of desolation through the forest, breaking against rocks, spilling into valleys and flowing over hills. A ravenous howling. The call of the Wild Hunt.

With the edge of his hand the Baron de Belleme slashed the space between himself and the hounds and loosed them into the night.

'I do try to understand him, I do—but times like this, I reckon he's lost his mind! What's he playing at, eh? Why does he think he can take a walk through Sherwood, at night, alone, with them mad animals out hunting?' Will felt betrayed, and angry at himself for not noticing that Robin had slipped away whilst they had still been debating what to do. 'I should've gone with him, to watch his back. They're cunning, them black wolves—evil! We can keep saying *Herne protect us* till we're blue in the face, but that won't help Robin if he can't find him.'

Marion was downcast, sitting on the ground by the campfire, trying to suppress the cough that had been aggravated by her repetitive attempts to defend Robin's strategy. After finally giving up, she had hugged close to Much, wrapped her cloak around them both, and laid a hand over his fist clasped tight around the hilt of Albion. Sharing his fears.

The sword hadn't left his grip since it had been placed into his care. Much had unsheathed the blade as soon as it was clear that Robin had left them, and he tried to concentrate on the firelight glimmering along the metal, turning the thought of flames into something good. All his trust was now invested in the strength and magic of the sword, preparing to fight creatures he didn't dare to imagine, and the overwhelming sense of duty rendered him mute.

Tuck and John sat back-to-back in unspoken support, with their strung bows and quivers resting across their laps; staying within the warmth of the fire but looking towards the darkness to make sure their night-vision wouldn't be ruined by the flickering yellow light. Justifications and recriminations were useless, so they refrained from engaging with Will, but they also knew he needed to vent his frustration, and so didn't attempt to calm him down, trusting that his anger would burn itself out. Waiting for him to accept the task they had been left with—to survive.

Nasir had taken up position on a rocky outcrop above the camp. His demeanour had transformed from compatriot to professional, and he'd removed himself from the others when they were still deep in dispute, unwilling to waste his energy. He had watched Robin leave whilst the others were distracted by the unearthly howling and had touched his forehead in salute. Robin had seen the gesture, nodded and raised his own hand before disappearing into the trees—Nasir knew it had been a tacit acknowledgement of the nature of their enemy.

In the chill of the English autumn breeze, he caught a fleeting scent of hot sand and perfumed air, a connecting filament stretched so thin it was hardly there anymore. The eyes of flame had shocked him into full awareness of the line that still ran from his heart to the golden, sweeping lands and azure skies of his birth—and the ancient, brooding supremacies, human and otherwise, that shared it. He settled, cross-legged and motionless, using the folds and fissures in the stone to disguise his shape, and held his scimitars poised in readiness, angled so they didn't reflect any firelight, as he stared into the night, mouthing prayers.

Tuck shifted position, easing his tense back. He spoke up softly during a lull in Will's tirade. 'The forest has gone quiet, have you noticed? Since those howls.'

'I have.' John pulled an arrow from his quiver and placed it alongside his bow. 'Everything's hiding. Everything *living*, that is.'

Finally, Will stopped pacing. He bent down to the woodpile and snatched up a branch. 'We need more torches—one fire's not enough to keep them wolves back.' His tone had changed; he sounded more controlled, and the fact he was suggesting practical responses to their plight was an encouraging sign. Tuck and John nudged each other in hope.

Nasir's voice came from the darkness above them. 'No, the jinn are not afraid of flame. It is their... essence?'

'Wait. Do you mean their souls? Or what they're made of?' John tried to grasp a concept that tested Nasir's ability to describe.

Tuck muttered under his breath. 'Those things have no souls. They're the devil's work.'

Nasir heard him. 'No. We are clay, they are fire. This world is their world, like us.'

Everyone fell silent, listening.

Nasir chose his next words carefully. 'They can be slaves and made to do evil—if a man has knowledge to bind them.'

John was the first to react, as the realisation of what Nasir was implying sent a shudder through him. 'Belleme? Is that who we're up against?' He rose to his feet, nocked the arrow to his string, but there was despair in his voice. 'We've no chance! None!'

'And Robin's out there! That's it—I'm getting him back.' Will went to fetch his bow and quiver, resolve dousing his anger.

Marion stood up. 'No! Please, we must stay here together, like he said—he knows what he's doing. We have to trust him.'

'Oh, I trust him all right—I just know he's wrong.' Will tightened his sword-belt and slung his quiver over his shoulder. He tried to walk past her to the path that led down into the trees, but she placed herself in his way. 'Marion,' he softened his manner, 'I'm doing this for you as well as for him.'

'I don't want you to—you heard what he said. You won't find him on the paths he'll be taking—I, *we* need you here.' Her emotions began to overwhelm her, and she had to fight to keep them contained. 'Please don't make me say it all *again*—I promised him, I—' she coughed, 'I promised—' then she couldn't stop.

Will dropped his weapons and stepped towards her to grab her into a hug. Tuck was already right behind, reaching out to support her. Between them, they lowered her back to the ground, closer to the warmth of the fire, as John brought a cup of water hastily poured from a leather pitcher. She sipped, spluttering, until the coughing stopped.

Much's face crumpled and tears ran down his cheeks, though he was careful not to make a sound.

'Alright, alright. I'll stay.' Will scowled, accepting defeat. 'But I'm telling you, *all* of you, if Robin's not back here by dawn, I'm going to find him, and if anything's happened to him, I'll cut the throat of every wolf in Sherwood till there's nothing left for them jinns to possess!'

John's hand went to his chest in a reflex of self-protection. In a moment of nightmarish empathy, he plummeted through a memory of being crushed into the tiniest space at the back of his mind by Belleme's sorcery; of having no control over the violence his body was compelled to perform. 'If Robin doesn't return, I'll be coming with you, Will—but you'll not be killing any poor beasts unless I say so.'

Abruptly, with clacking beaks and a flurry of unseen wings, the ravens abandoned their roost in the cliff and took flight, cawing in alarm. Before anyone could react, the fire dimmed; the flames cooling to a blue-tinged yellow, embers greying to ash. The bright circle of its heat contracted, sucking the blackness into the camp.

Nasir called out from the rock face above them. 'Eyes! Red eyes!'

They spun around to face a night that was suddenly as solid as a dungeon wall around them—but saw nothing. Then, a pair of glowing orbs appeared, still some way in the distance. They seemed to blink as they weaved between trees invisible in the gloom of the forest, yet no one doubted that the stare was as fixed as the north star.

Tuck broke their enthralled dismay. 'Build up the fire, don't let it go out!' He pulled up the small wooden cross he wore, kissed it and slipped it back next to his heart, then trotted to the woodpile and began flinging the driest branches onto the dying campfire.

John shook himself, consciously sloughing the weight of the lingering trauma; there was enough horror without dragging more from his mind. He stood beside Tuck and heaved the largest deadwood limb from the pile, raised it like a club and smashed it into splinters that he threw onto the fire. The kindling caught immediately, giving a momentary sense of elation before winking out again.

Will, sword in hand, knelt down to blow on the embers, but was soon gasping and out of breath, to no avail.

Much stood in trepidation, hugging Albion to his chest, unable to move.

'More eyes! Another jinn!' Nasir loosed an arrow to signal the direction. He knew there was no chance of hitting his target yet.

The others looked to where the arrow had been lost, then spotted eyes to their right, at least a mile from the first pair. The creatures must have been hunting alone, homing in on their prey independently.

'At least we can see them coming with them always staring at us.' Will had given up on saving the fire to take up position on the edge of the escarpment. He put his sword away and loaded his longbow, waiting for a mark. 'The bastards can't find us with their eyes shut...' He looked over at John, who had come to stand beside him with his own bow. '...Can they?' He raised his voice as loud as he dared, calling to Nasir. '*Can they?*'

There was a long pause in which Will and John stared at each other in fearful doubt.

'No. They see, like we see.' Nasir replied, finally.

They let out their held breaths.

Marion did her best to nurture the campfire, but no matter how carefully she arranged the scraps of wood, they just charred without catching alight. When she touched the ashes, she found they were as cold as the frosty ground. Marion ringed the fire with logs to protect it from the breeze, yet still it shrank away. Her pale face was ghostly, hollowed by the weakening glow.

'Leave it, little flower.' Tuck gently took her smudged hand and raised her up. 'We have to put our faith in God and arrows now.'

PART 9

Robin knew the forest paths by heart, but he carried a lantern with all but one of its parchment panels blacked out by mud, to help see the ground directly ahead. Frost had taken hold and stars of ice caught the candlelight. He traversed the inclines, the basins of marshy ground, the dense stands of saplings, and the deer-coppiced glades, tilting his longbow to prevent it snagging on branches. Here and there, the fallen trunks of old trees blocked or diverted him onto animal trails, hoof-thin tracks, navigated one foot in line with the other, so as not to lose his way. A few of the ancient oaks along his route were cut with a sigil, most old and healed to ridges bisecting creases in the bark, found only by touch. Others—the ones he sought—were freshly cut, their arrow and antler shapes acting as faint beacons in the darkness.

Anyone else would have been hopelessly lost, but Robin had learned these pathways as a boy, running and playing in a realm that he ruled with carefree innocence. Those years had given him a natural affinity for the deep woods, and taught lessons he put into practice now.

He was heading for the places that used to strike fear into him as a child—places that were under a timeless protection beyond his understanding, and always held him back from exploring further. Respect for the land had been drummed into him by a shiver on a warm day, a prickle over his skin, the feeling of being watched. There would be sounds he couldn't identify as coming from any animal he knew; a keening wail on the fluting wind, and a stuttering drumbeat felt through the soles of his feet. Never any tales he could run home and tell and achieve anything other than ridicule for his perceived faintheartedness—but he knew the enchantment was real, and that he was being kept away from places he had no business entering. And so he had studied them from afar, fearful and fascinated, until the responsibilities of adulthood took him away.

For a while.

He found the tight turn, doubling back on itself, luring those without trust to abandon the true track.

A gap winding through a thicket of blackthorn, to be walked upright and unflinching.

A steep slope where the path dropped into a gully.

Robin grabbed rope-twists of trailing ivy and used them to lower himself down the outcrops of stone that created an uneven stairway. He was nearing the place he knew as a sanctuary—one of the frightening places he had avoided as a boy. Holding the lantern high, he spotted a scar, cut into the trunk of an oak and shining with sap. He went to it, and with reverence, traced the form with his finger: a stylised arrow recut over previously healed incisions.

He was close to his destination.

Robin became aware of movement behind him, and thinking he was being met on the path, almost called out—then realised that he'd allowed himself to be distracted by reminiscences. The quiet tread was not that of Herne coming to greet him. It was the deliberate precision of a stalking animal. He threw the lantern as far as he could to one side and circled behind the oak, slipping an arrow from his quiver and nocking it in a single motion. With the greatest care he leaned around the tree, straining to see what was following him, to pick out a form from the endless shades and layers of the nighttime forest.

A shifting branch? A crevice between rocks? A moving shadow? Robin's fingers tightened on the bowstring.

Two silk-thin lines of red appeared in the furthest gloom.

Opened wide.

As if it understood that there was nothing more to be gained by staying hidden, the creature peeled off from the shadows to reveal itself: a huge black hound, darker than the night, head swaying as it sniffed the freezing air. Its eyes twin tunnels into hell.

And with a sick dread in his gut, Robin realised that he had led it to Herne's stronghold.

The flow of the breeze entering the cavern changed. The scents it carried of the autumn richness and rot were replaced by a sharp tang of charred fur, of the stink of sulphur and burnt flesh. Herne held his hand into the stream of air and twisted his fingers in the filaments: many had found a way to burrow into the earth, rock and trees. Some tendrils reached for a connection that didn't exist, and those ones flailed, unable to attach to the locus into which they'd been released. The strongest twined around the oncoming winter and its mercilessness—those were the ones that struck fear into him.

He let his arms drop to his sides, and his bare feet blend with the stone floor. The cold of the dying season had already penetrated him to his bones; he was ready to withdraw into the deepest places and dream with the earth until spring, holding the lines and the lore of the land safe in the bedrock of his body. It was a wrench to have to break the gentle crusts of ice he had allowed to grow in white ferns over his skin. They melted in the warmth of his resurgent blood, running over and breaking the spirals of ochre on his body.

He sensed the call before he heard it. His name and his role, a pure concept borne above and untouched by the foulness. He had no choice but to answer.

A father's duty.

The significance awakened his humanity and its animal simplicity: to love, to protect, to survive and pass on the knowledge and stories that sustained life, spirit and purpose. He took a long breath and began to shiver as he became conscious of the chill, there was no time to prepare—he had to drag himself from the depths of his mind and reclaim his mortal form. His tunic and cloak lay on the ground, rimed with frost. He picked them up, shook them and the ice crystals sparked in the firelight. He pulled the clothing on, tied the lacings and belt. The antlered headdress was set upon a simple wooden alter, encircled with loops of strung hawthorn berries. He lifted and placed it upon his head—and fully awake, the terror of the hunt surged through him.

Herne snatched up the silver arrow from its place under the alter, unwrapped it from its deerskin covering and placed it inside his tunic—the metal so cold against his chest, it burned—and he ran for the cave entrance.

Outside, the night was a blank, and his sight took a moment to adjust to the darkness of the forest. His instincts told him to stand still and listen. He heard an arrow being shot, then another and looked to where they were striking into branches—saw a pair of blood-red eyes, higher from the ground than even the tallest wolf's could be, veering as the creature dodged the shafts.

Herne backed away, trusting his bare feet to make no sound. He swathed himself in the thoughts of the trees so he would be hidden amongst them. The eyes remained fixated elsewhere—his son was close; the arrows were his: streaks of fervour slicing the cold air. And then they stopped. There was a shout—his name and a warning together—and Robin ran to his side, ready to shoot again to protect him, but the older man pushed his bow arm down.

'You cannot kill it.'

Robin couldn't look away from the approaching glare. 'How do I stop it? Tell me!'

'Heed me.' Herne's voice was calm and so at odds with the threat that Robin turned. He couldn't make out any features beneath the stag's head cowl, but the shadow was a benign place, a refuge from the dread. 'This thing knows your arrows—it can avoid them because it has felt the cut of your iron before.'

Robin recalled the attack in the glade, the random shots sent after the beasts. The one cry of an animal wounded.

Herne raised his head, revealing his face. 'But it is not the only hunter in the forest.'

A faint rumble grew from the ground and reverberated in the furthest reaches of the cavern at their backs: a drumming growing rapidly louder, the crash of branches stamped and tossed aside.

The thunder of cloven hooves breached the treeline above the sanctuary in a burst of noise that sent them both cowering with arms raised above their heads. A stag leapt from the ridge in an arc over them—felt more than seen—in a rush of power and the stench of an animal in terror. It hit the ground and sprang away into the darkness.

Before they could crouch back under shelter, a dozen more harts and hinds in a tight herd launched above them, scattering soil and gravel, pounding the earth as they landed and bolted for the thickets.

The disturbance had been so visceral that Robin somehow expected the red eyes to have been swept away in the tumult. The deer had galloped right through where he had last seen the beast's glare, and surely no animal, however strange its nature, could have endured being trampled by such a force? He looked to Herne for confirmation, but instead was shown where the eyes were slit, close to the forest floor, rising. Creeping forward again.

Just as Robin raised his bow—compelled to resist even though he knew it was useless—more sounds came from behind. This time there was a softer but no less powerful impact of running feet, the scrape of claws, heavy panting; a gap in the rhythm as forms jumped from the higher ground to the slopes below; bodies barrelling over them, twisting, bracing to land and bounding away.

And then came a scream, the terrible cry first heard back at the camp. Robin shuddered, repulsed.

In response the wolves howled, a rallying call that told of an enemy that must be challenged, even at the expense of losing the prey they were pursuing. The pack swerved abruptly towards the shrieks, in a snarling wave ready to break.

A chance of deliverance—Robin willed them to attack.

Herne thrust a hand inside his ragged mantle and pressed the silver arrow tight to his skin. The beat of his heart sang in the silver.

The wolves swarmed over the dark shape and the burning eyes disappeared. The growls rose in pitch, became frantic, the glow reignited and swelled, the shapes of the wolves were silhouetted against the incandescence as they struggled to bite at a foe that had melted into a featureless sphere of heat.

'Help them!' Robin grabbed for Herne's arm— and it felt like he'd grasped at the limb of a tree, as if he stood beside an oak caught in the wavering light of a wildfire. There was no sign of face or form beneath the cloak—the man he knew had gone beyond his reach.

A paw… Running across the cave walls, the twisting passageways, he guided the pack through the dark. It ran with the oncoming cold, bringing it up from the deep, and winter was caught in their fur and blown out of their jaws.

A freezing wind knocked Robin to the ground. On hands and knees, he scrambled closer to the protection of Herne's stolid, invulnerable form, as the blast travelled the same path as the deer and the wolves, hurtling over their heads.

It reached the desperate pack and swirled around them. Within the haze of ice and mist, Robin thought he could see the outlines of more wolves: the living animals multiplied by simpler shapes drawn around them in an earthier red than the glow they fought.

Their yelps lowered into growls, a menacing, confident threat, and the roiling bodies—of life and of spirit—steadied into a tightening ring of bared fangs and bunched muscles. The deadlock was broken by the light flaring, a defiance that triggered the wolves to pounce. As they closed in for the kill, the red orb dwindled into two eyes, and Robin saw them fix upon him the instant before they winked out altogether.

Howls of triumph soared through the abrupt darkness. The wind carrying the spectral wolves dissipated into the trees, and with snuffing, yips and snapping teeth, the living pack followed.

Herne staggered forward; all his unyielding sturdiness gone. Robin reacted just in time to catch and support him. When he was able to straighten up, Herne slid the silver arrow from its place by his enduring heart and held it up to the night skies, where it gathered the faint starlight and blazed into a brand of white fire.

A paw, an arrow, a flame...

PART 10

The Baron de Belleme flinched. He rubbed his gloved hands over his face, momentarily muffling his quiet chanting. His expression remained neutral though, and there appeared to be no effort being expended in the process of summoning his hound. It was second nature, an easy fetch, and he tempted the dog to answer more quickly by offering the scent of charred flesh tossed into the leaf litter. He felt for the connection, pulled it tight, and reeled in the notion of a line of flame.

Suddenly, the ground before him began to bulge, pressed up from below, and where the soil cracked, a jagged, molten glow escaped, illuminating his surroundings. The black hound erupted, shook itself free of the clods of earth, and laid down at Belleme's feet.

He removed his gloves, tucked them in his belt, and bent to stroke its thick pelt. He ran his hand along the dog's spine and down to the wound on its haunch. The blood, hidden by the fur, had dried, and when he pressed his fingertips to the cut, he could feel the shape of the broken arrowhead under its skin. The dog didn't flinch, but when Belleme grasped its scruff, it squinted in fear. He pulled back the hound's head to examine its eyes, scrying for information within their glowing ruby mirrors.

What he saw elicited a thin-lipped, calculating smile. He let go of the dog and brushed his hands clean. He took a moment to analyse his next move, contemplating the night sky between the crowns of the trees. It was velvet blue, stars scintillating with a clarity that only came with the colder months.

Belleme knew the onset of winter was the advantage that he needed. A god bound to the rhythms of the forest would be in retreat, and everything and everyone protected by that waning influence would become vulnerable; a season when the hunt could pick off the weak. It was a pitiless yet noble calling. There was no benefit to man or beast in allowing inferiority to proliferate. It was his duty to usurp the primitive regents and to establish a throne—one deeply rooted in the land's powers—for the majesty of his lord and master Azael.

And his sceptre would be the silver arrow.

At the click of his fingers, Belleme's horse trotted up to him, tossing its head, nostrils flared, caught between obedience and its fear of the hound. The Baron snatched the reins, swung up into the saddle and pointed to the ground at his side. As the dog padded up, awaiting the next command, his horse trembled and sidestepped, and he had to whisper a calming word. It stilled as if turned to stone.

At the next signal, the hound set off, nose to the earth, noisily huffing at the myriad scents. It ploughed its muzzle into the leaf litter, sweeping it from side to side, then found the trace it knew and leapt ahead. Belleme kicked his spurs into his horse and urged it into pursuit. The gloom was no hindrance to the otherworldly senses of the black dog, and provided Belleme cantered close and kept his head below the curve of the horse's neck, he was sure to avoid overhanging branches. Soon, the ambient light increased as they negotiated a shallow incline towards outcrops of stony ground and turf, where the trees were thinned by browsing deer and wandering livestock. The moon began to rise, a half-lidded eye staring blindly over the horizon, but the running hound remained a depthless void, untouched by the brightness.

From far ahead, on the highest ridge that broke from the treeline, Belleme could hear the vestiges of shouts, almost lost in the breeze that carried them and under the pounding of his horse's hooves. They might have been dismissed as a shepherd calling his flock or poachers pushing their luck, but for the faint, intermittent belling of hunting hounds.

His unleashed dogs had the Wolfsheads at bay.

Robin and Herne stood on the place where the fiery spectre had vanished. The earth was churned up by the digging claws of the wolf pack and the hooves of the stampeding deer. At the centre was a depression of burnt ground, stinking of charred leaves and twigs, where tendrils of smoke were still rising from the soil. Curious, Robin bent down to touch the blackened circle, but Herne grabbed him.

'No, don't give it any more connections it can use.'

'I thought the wolves killed it.' Robin stood up and stepped back a pace. 'Isn't that why it disappeared?' He held his bow across his body like a staff.

'Such creatures do not need to die to change form.'

'Then I have to make sure it doesn't find its way to the camp—tell me where it is!'

'I cannot... it is quickened fire; I am slow rivers of ice. It knows I am bound by the heaviness of winter.' Herne lifted his cowl and let the stag's head fall backwards. The weight dragged the cloak from his shoulders, and his tattered mantle and the downward-pointing antlers made him seem nothing more than a broken tree resigned to falling.

Robin was appalled by the capitulation. He fully understood the changes that the seasons wrought on his mentor, and the roles he had to fulfil; older responsibilities than the ones owed to him. Yet Herne had seemed at the height of his power when he raised the silver arrow over the exultant wolves— now that energy had drained down into the earth again, leaving him hollow.

Herne still held the arrow. He lifted his head to look at Robin, fatigue in the bark-creases on his face, his eyes dim. 'Only one thing is clear to me— you must bear the arrow while I am in this state of dwindling, ward it until the chill in my blood hardens to ice, and my strength returns with the longest night.'

'I promised Marion I would bring it back with me, but that was before I saw what we're fighting against—how can I keep it any safer than it would be with you?'

'Because, my son, you are equal to the fire that hunts us.'

His words resonated through the ground. It was a declaration that brooked no protest. Robin bowed his head.

'You must go. The darkness is closing in on those you love.' Herne took Robin's hand and placed the heavy silver arrow upon his palm. 'Do your duty—to them, and to me.'

Robin tensed his grip around the cold edges, pressing their pattern into his skin. Allowing no time for doubt, he slipped the arrow into his quiver and set off at once. As it nestled between the wood, the moon caught the metal, briefly consecrating his humble arrows with its white light.

Herne raised his hands in blessing—his arms were bare branches, his hair was strands of lichen, his torso was the ivy-wound trunk of an oak.

When Robin reached the rise that would take him out of sight, he turned to wave farewell, but the woodland was still, and the only shapes were those of the trees.

Robin retraced his path. It was easier now that the moon had risen, though it cast deceptive shadows that snagged his attention as he ran. He checked for the silhouettes of dogs or wolves, and for the demonic red eyes. All he saw were the occasional tinges of ethereal green from the toadstools and fungus growing on rotting logs, the spangled reflection of the sky in pools and streams, and the glint of the frost. His inbreaths seared his lungs with the cold and blew out as vapour. His legs pounded the uneven ground; he vaulted logs, clambered up rocks, sprinted across clearings, sweating despite the chill.

Then, he heard the sound he'd been dreading. Drifting from the uplands came a howl. He stopped to listen. Another howl, a different direction. He wiped his face, trying to judge their course so he could choose a route to take. The howls roughened to a sonorous baying, destroying any hope that it was the wolves. Dangerous as they were, he could deal with them, but the dogs were being directed to serve a malevolent mind that Robin had no way of fathoming.

There was no option but to race the hounds to the camp and pray that he would be able to use his knowledge of the terrain to pass by unnoticed, whilst they focused on their target.

Though it was still far off, the barking intensified—then slid into undulating howls interspersed with the unmistakable cries of his companions: shouts and silences that corresponded to the timing of a volley of arrows. Robin took heart from the fact they were defending themselves—but knew if the dogs were within range, he was already too late.

PART 11

'They're closing in!' Will snatched another arrow from the diminishing pile between him and John. He nocked and pulled to full draw, sighting down the shaft to the pair of red eyes set in a dark form beginning to ascend the slopes below their campsite. 'How in *hell* has none of us hit 'em?'

Tuck drew his arrow. 'The answer lies in your question.'

'*Loose!*' Will gave the command.

Three arrows hissed into the shadows of the scrubland, all adjusted for the drop and the anticipated direction the creature was taking. Once again, their shots were wasted, lost in the bracken, thorns and birch.

With no time for frustration, they loaded their bows, aiming at the second pair of approaching eyes.

'*Loose!*' Hammering heartbeats. Peering into the darkness… arrows clattering against boulders and brush-wood.

The eyes blinked and continued their ascent.

Marion held her bow tight against her, hugging it for support. She studied the landscape laid out before them; a tapestry of dismal shades, stitched with silver picked out by the moon and stars. Her watch was for Robin though, and she hardly spared a glance at the dogs. Much positioned himself in front of her, with Albion held out in readiness, inadvertently blocking her view and she had to lean away from him to see.

The sword blade shone in the moonlight, and Marion was seized by the imagery. A memory stirred. For a held breath, she was clutched by the heat-flash of fever, hearing her name being called.

'Marion?'

Much's worried whisper right in her ear snatched her back into the cold night. He still held the sword steady, despite his shivering, but all his attention was on her.

'I'm alright.' Marion was shocked at the weakness of her voice. She coughed and tried again. 'Keep looking. He'll be here soon.' She planted her feet more steadily. 'I know he will.'

With a pattering of grit, then a soft scuffing of boots landing on the stone behind her, Nasir left his eyrie to join them. The hounds were so close now, there was no advantage in observing from the additional height. His scimitars were sheathed, his bow readied. Although he hadn't condemned the decision, he'd chosen not to shoot with the others after observing the behaviour of the dogs, to save his arrows for when they might be of more use.

He stepped up beside Marion and pointed to a place on the ragged border of the forest where the mature trees thinned. 'There—it is him.'

Marion's heart leapt. She strained to see what Nasir indicated, moving closer to him so she could sight down his arm, and then she spotted what could easily have been dismissed as branches swaying in the wind, but Nasir's skill had filtered the random shifting from the stealthy, conscious movement.

It was too dark to make out any details on the figure, yet she knew it was Robin. She was torn, willing him to run towards her—craving him—and also wanting him to remain safe in the forest, far from the dogs.

Nasir sensed her inner conflict. 'Trust him, he will come. The jinn do not see he is behind them; they look only at us.' He gave her a reassuring smile, took an arrow from his quiver and nocked it. 'We will make sure they look nowhere else.' He joined his companions at the ridge.

Marion shivered from the chill and the tension. The figure slipped from one patch of black to the next, and she wished she could call out to urge him on, or to take cover, depending on the manoeuvrings of the eyes. Robin couldn't see them from where he was, and she worried that he would inadvertently overtake the hounds. In effect, a rough chessboard had been laid out on the monochrome slopes below, and she had no choice but to witness the moves without being able to help.

'*Loose!*' The next volley clattered on a pavement of bare stone to the side of one dog: a deliberate miss to herd the creature closer to its fellow.

'*Loose!*' Their arrows went wide again—this time, the other dog was steered by the thud of arrows into a hawthorn grove beside it.

Nasir had observed that direct aims were being avoided by the hounds hunkering flat to the ground—almost melting into it—and oblique shots by shifting sideways. Buoyed by this breakthrough, they guarded Robin's path, but with every volley, the black dogs were coming closer. The bulk of their bodies could now be distinguished from the coarse ground and the glare of their eyes sheened their muzzles. They were massive, relentless, and terrifyingly solid.

'Much! We need your arrows,' John called out, reaching back without turning around.

Much hesitated, unsure of what to do with Albion, before fumbling the sword into one hand so he could pass his full quiver over.

'Do you need mine too?' Marion began to lift her quiver from her belt.

Tuck held up his palm. 'No, little flower, you keep them for yourself—just in case.'

His sad half-smile, intended to be encouraging, had the opposite effect, and all Marion could read in his expression was resignation. She swallowed down the threat of tears and scanned the landscape for Robin.

There was no sign of him. She looked to where he had last crossed between boulders, noting that the stark shadows cast by the moon had softened. The light, such as it was, seemed to be bleeding over the ground, and she realised that a mist was rolling out from the treeline—he must be using it as concealment. The hounds were being steered across to the steepest approach, leaving the way open to the slopes that she and Much surveyed. Marion's hand went to her arrows by reflex, stroked the fletchings, pulled one out. She steeled herself to shoot.

A change in the flow of the mist caught her attention, a swirl of disturbance, closer than she dared to anticipate. A figure stood up from the haze and she knew him immediately. Marion had to clamp her hand over her mouth to stop herself from calling his name. She gripped Much's sleeve and put a finger to his lips, before pointing Robin out.

Much gasped and took a step to the very brink of the ridge. In silence, he held Albion aloft, and there was a nobility to his stance that came from a source much deeper than stolen titles and brutal victories.

Marion tugged his arms back down, nervous that the gesture could alert the hounds to Robin's location, but she hugged him, and they shared a brief smile of communion.

The mist closed in and thickened, in an unnerving wave of whiteness billowing across the lower ground. They saw Robin allow it to envelop him and turn the ghostly advance into deliverance.

The arrows kept flying into the night, and the hounds were forced closer together. They never changed pace or flinched when the shafts shattered onto the ground beside them; they just took a measured sidestep, allowing themselves to be driven, their eyes flaming brighter and their shaggy bodies resolving from the dark as they neared.

'They're not stopping.' With considerable effort, John kept his voice steady. 'I'm nearly out of arrows.'

Tuck fitted his last shaft to the string. 'We've done what was needed—the way's clear for Robin, thank the Lord.' This time, he didn't wait for Will's signal and with an indulgent flash of anger, he aimed it straight at the eyes. As before, the dogs gave the impression of sinking into the earth to avoid the shot, then rising to continue their inexorable prowl.

Taking his cue from Tuck, Will loosed an arrow towards the hounds in what should have been an easy kill. It skimmed the bracken, passed harmlessly over the creatures' heads, and on into the bank of mist. 'Fall back! When they get up here, form up with swords and staffs—any arrows left, give 'em to Marion.'

Nasir dropped back from the shooting line, threw his bow aside and drew his scimitars.

John backed away; jaw gritted in frustration. His quarterstaff was near the ashes of the campfire and, as he went to fetch it, he passed Marion. 'Stay behind us. Don't fret, we'll keep them away from you.' He touched her arm. 'Save your arrows till we've done everything we can... Don't waste them.' The intensity of his expression conveyed an ominous implication. Marion bit her lip, then gave a nod to show she understood.

Much was still watching the leading edge of the fog bank swirling and roiling like a slow incoming sea. He appeared not to have heard anything that had been said, and when John went up to him, he flinched, startled from his sentinel trance.

'We need you and Albion with us.' John kept his tone as gentle as he could, hating how his words drained the optimism from Much's face.

'But Robin's nearly here!'

'The dogs already are.' A rising snarl from them punctuated his statement. He encircled Much's shoulders and took him where the hound's eyes below them turned the rock red as the glow from a forge. 'Stay by me, lad. We'll guard each other's backs.'

'Not dogs—*demons*.' Much's voice was so plaintive it was hard for John to hear—and even harder to bear.

Tuck, Will and Nasir had placed themselves a sword-length from each other, allowing for a swing to not accidentally strike a companion. Much joined them and John took one pace in front, with his staff held at the ready.

'What we need is shields.' Will muttered as he raised his sword, hilt by his cheek, pointing the tip down towards the scrabbling noise of claws raking over stone.

'God's grace will be our shield-wall.' Tuck stated with more certainty than he felt, planting his feet firmly to steady his own blade.

The amen poised on John's lips was blown away by a sudden blast of wind. With a roar, the two black dogs leapt up onto the ridge, dagger teeth bared, eyes blazing. Any remnant of the ordinary hounds they had been was gone; the things that clawed at the rock, snarling, were monsters bloated with fire and fury.

John, channelling his shock into a yell of rage, thrust his quarterstaff at the closest dog, putting all his strength into the lunge, but instead of taking a blow that should have crushed its rib cage, it sprang upwards and jumped over their heads to land behind them. They were now fighting on two sides—and Marion was in the gravest danger.

Before Will could shout a warning, Nasir ran to stand between her and the hound, slashing at its gaping jaws. It snapped at the blades and backed off a pace, but there was no indication of distress in its behaviour, only an evaluation of the threats it was facing.

Marion, though terrified, darted from behind him and shot an arrow at the dog's face. Point-blank range, a faultless aim, and yet she missed. The creature snapped at the arrow, caught and crunched it to splinters that fell from its slavering mouth. Nasir advanced on it, scimitars catching the red and the white light of the flaming eyes and the moon. He brought down his blades to slash the dog's throat.

Tuck had fallen trying to follow Nasir. He now crawled through the mayhem of yells and curses, pushing his sword ahead across the stone, desperate to reach Marion.

John was jabbing his staff at the other hound, distracting and keeping it away from Will, who was attempting to dodge behind to stab at its hindquarters. Much was holding Albion in two hands, waving it with all his might and copied skill, teeth clenched with the determination to control the blade and his terror.

The first wave had been of heat, the second was of freezing cold—the fog tide rose and breached their small plateau, and the greyness swirled around them, cutting what dim illumination they had from the night sky. The dogs were huge black shapes, lunging from the mist, their growls and the clamour of battle muffled. The ground became slick with condensation, boots and claws sliding on the rock. The hounds' lurid eyes were floating fires in the murk, constant and unassailable.

Tuck reached Marion. He stood up beside her, one arm keeping her behind the protection of his body, and then joined Nasir's attack.

A figure materialised on the far side of the camp, moving with the flow of the mist towards the fighters. Much noticed its approach and gasped with relief, letting his burning muscles rest, dropping Albion's blade tip to touch the stone. 'Robin! It's Robin!'

The cry snatched everyone's attention, even the hounds paused their assault, and then they started to back away, huge heads lowered in obeisance, red eyes narrowed—and for a heartbeat, the outlaws believed that Robin had vanquished them.

But when the fog parted around the figure, like a swirling silken curtain, the Baron de Belleme emerged. From the concealment of his robes stalked the third black dog, eyes ablaze, long yellowed teeth bared in a fiendish, mocking grin.

The other hounds fell in beside it, tongues lolling, panting from the strain of combat.

Despair sapped the outlaws of their strength—they could no longer force themselves to defy Belleme's conjured desolation.

The Baron looked around dispassionately and adopted a sympathetic tone. 'Has your petty forest god abandoned you? Is he withering like the dying leaves?' Then his expression hardened, and he bellowed, 'The fires I bring will burn for eternity! The light of Azael is *never* extinguished!' The three hounds raised their voices with his and howled long and piercingly. He clicked his fingers, and they stopped instantly. 'And where is Herne's serf-son, your peasant leader?' He leaned forward to scrutinise the six faces, rapt with dread, staring back at him. 'Your woodland *king*?'

'I'm here.'

Robin's voice, calm and steady, came from the mist, and the smothered echoes from the rocks scattered it, so that its origin couldn't be discerned.

Belleme flinched, his gaze darting, seeing nothing. 'Then you truly are a fool.' He controlled himself, and with a hissed word sent the dogs to find him.

Knowing Robin was with them transformed the mood of his companions; from the bleakness of defeat to resolve in an instant. They still had to force themselves against the chill that bit into their bones, making their actions painfully clumsy, but they shuffled back as far as they dared to the brink of the steepest drop that couldn't be climbed—even by the monstrous dogs—and bunched close together, weapons bristling outwards like the hackles of the hounds hunting Robin.

The dogs bounded off, seeking a scent, the glare of their eyes like flaming torches lighting the mist, their dark bulk veiled then magnified by turns as the creatures paced back and forth through the churning earth-bound clouds. All that could be heard was the scratch of claws raking the stone, growls and snorted breaths, becoming more rapid as the pursuit degenerated into a frenzy that betrayed how well Robin was evading them.

Belleme spoke into the mist, his words hushed the dogs. They were murky, hunched shapes, looming larger as they turned from their evidently futile task to one that would prove more productive. He calmly raised his hand and pointed at Marion. 'Take the girl.'

The outlaws reacted by bundling her behind them and facing the oncoming threat with their swords outstretched. John, at the fore because of his reach, braced his quarterstaff and brandished the end at the advancing hounds.

Will whispered, 'If they get past John, stab 'em in the eyes—if they can't see, they can't get her.'

'They've used their devilry to avoid getting shot. What if they can dodge our swords, too?' Tuck's belief was faltering in the growing red glare. As the dogs padded closer, the fog was lit by their eyes, and Belleme loomed nebulous and threatening as a thunderhead behind them.

Marion, cramped at the back, elbows almost pinned to her sides, was trying to fumble an arrow onto her string. Her heels scuffed the lip of the ridge, sending pebbles clattering into the drop. 'Let me get to the front where I can shoot.' Her distress turning to frustration. 'Even if they can't be hit, at least I can keep them away from you.'

Nasir leaned close so only she could hear. 'No. You are bait—it is Robin he wants.'

The quiet reason in his words stopped her. The strong backs of the men in front of her were the last barrier between her and tragedy. She folded her arms around her bow but didn't put the arrow away. Nasir inclined his head in thanks then turned to face the prowling dogs.

They seemed to have grown, emboldened by their master's direction. Their eyes were globes of concentrated fire ready to melt from their sockets.

The fog ribboned as they closed in, shrinking from the touch of their bodies as if burned away, and a clear semicircle opened up where they walked, stinking of the hot, sulphurous air gusted from the creatures' jaws. They tested the defences by snapping at the swords and the staff, easily avoiding the outlaws' answering lunges.

John noted the slight limp in the gait of the largest hound. If Robin was to have a chance of outflanking the Baron, he knew they would need to initiate the clash—waiting for Belleme to choose his time would hand him the advantage. So, without warning, and knowing his companions would understand and follow his lead, John thrust the point of his quarterstaff to its fullest reach, straight into the hind leg of the wounded dog.

A piercing scream burst from the creature. It fell on its back, skidding across the rock from the force of the blow. It struggled up, dragging its leg, snarling with rage. Immediately, the other hounds flew at the outlaws, mouths agape, to be met with slashing steel. The injured dog joined in the attack, undaunted by its broken leg, carried by the strength of its desire to kill. John swung at it as soon as it was within range, the impact jarring his arms, but the dog kept advancing until it caught the staff in its teeth, and with a snarl, wrenched it from his grip and bit it in two. Cursing his torn muscles, John pulled his dagger and retreated to within the protection of the swords.

The Baron de Belleme, wreathed in fog and blending into the angles of the rock face, didn't bother to check the progress of his pack; his whole attention was on the surrounding jagged summit. There was no sign of Robin in the Hood—evidently the threat to his pitiable woodland wife had not been a sufficient inducement to show himself.

No matter. The Lord Azael provided connections that *could* be used.

He closed his eyes and shaped the thought of a filament of sand, spun from a single grain, reaching out from his fingertip toward the battling Wolfsheads.

Slowly and precisely, mouthing an incantation, he drew an inverse pentagram in the air.

John—now only armed with a knife—backed up to where he could be of most use as a second line of defence behind the swords. He did contemplate taking Albion from Much but knew that it was better used to support the younger man's courage. His short blade and long reach would have to suffice.

Marion, who was crouched and flinching, her gaze darting from one vicious dog to the next as they lunged for her, was very grateful for his reassuring bulk beside her.

The protective arm he had placed around her shoulders tightened, and she accepted the sudden pressure, thinking he was tugging her away from the snapping jaws of the hounds—but his grip became a vice that stifled her, and her eyes widened in horrified disbelief as she felt the cold blade of his dagger press against her throat.

John clamped his hand over her mouth and lifted her. She kicked furiously but could do nothing to stop him from backing out of the protection of the ring of swords. He took her at a run—before anyone could react—into the wall of fog from where he was being summoned. The agonising five-pointed star on the skin of his chest easing as he yielded to its demand.

There was only pain in his body and numbness in his mind. He watched himself from afar, incorporeal as the mist, as he wrestled Marion towards the Baron, with tears he could not feel, running down his face.

Will stabbed at the exposed neck of one of the dogs as it made a grab for Much. The yelp and spurt of blood should have indicated a killing blow, but these animals were infused with a diabolical endurance, and received cut after cut with no more than a cry and renewed ferocity. He sliced at the next dog, scoring its chest as it jumped out of his range and into Nasir's, who took it on, scimitars thrashing. In that brief break, Will checked behind for Marion and John—and was immediately transfixed by the empty gap where they should have been. 'Where are they? Where are they!' The alarm in his tone was infectious; the others turned, too.

'Have... they fallen?' Tuck, gasping, landed a kick on a hound's snout, followed it up with a stab, and shoved his way to the edge of the ridge. He was met by blank fog. He leaned out as far as he could to shout their names, listened for an answer, called again and his voice seemed louder—the clamour of the battle had ceased.

The three black dogs backed off, sword gashes dripping blood, patches of fur torn to the flesh, panting hard, still snarling and remorseless. The exhausted outlaws huddled, their chests heaving, their sword-arms aching, with bloody rips in their clothes from glancing claws and fangs.

'Have we won?' Much whispered.

'No.' Sorrow choked Tuck, and he could say no more.

Belleme's voice rang out, sonorous and compelling. 'Robin in the Hood! I offer you a simple exchange—one that even a murderous peasant should be able to comprehend!'

Though no answer came, the feeling of attentiveness was intense. The Baron smiled to himself.

'Give yourself up and I will let your woman live!' He wound his fingers through the air as if reeling in an invisible thread. John, staring blankly with Marion struggling against his grip, stepped out from the fog to stand beside him. The hounds joined them and lay down to lick their wounds but remained vigilant, never closing their burning eyes, and the mist surrounding them was stained with their red light.

Robin clenched his jaw against the impulse to call out to Marion, to tell her he was close and to not be afraid. He had to be steadfast. Though the terror of facing a resurrected enemy was gouging out his courage, his conflicted thoughts were suddenly hushed by the forest; with the sensation of standing among the trees, deep-rooted and high-reaching, remembering how hollowed oaks could still withstand blow after blow of winter for generations, and arise green again.

Nothing's forgotten…

The Silver Arrow was the light keeping the leaves alive, healing the breach in his heart torn by doubt.

Nothing is ever forgotten.

Robin could only see the vaguest shapes of the gathering, John's silhouette being the most obvious from where Robin advanced. His height and build were an ideal cover, and the Baron would naturally assume that no threat could come from that direction—even so, Robin knew he had to be quick as a fox before his scent reached the hounds.

He crept closer. *Herne, guide me!*

Robin leapt out, carving the silver arrow down through the mist in front of John's chest. Though he didn't touch his friend's body or snag his clothes, Robin felt the resistance and give of something being severed. The arrow flared for a second, as if reflecting a desert sun, but he bore the pain and kept his fist tight around the scorching metal, pointing it towards Belleme.

John let out a wail of anguish. He released Marion, dropped the dagger he was holding to her neck, and scrubbed in anger and disgust at the searing memory of the pentagram on his chest. Marion staggered, gasping and clutching her throat, as Robin stepped between her and the Baron.

Straining to regain his senses, hauling back his sense of self, John shouted for the others whilst desperately casting about for anything he could use as a weapon. Marion kept her emotions in check, surreptitiously rubbing sensation back into her numbed hands so she could be ready and able to load her bow. The discomfort of having it clamped against her body when she was seized, was a price she was now glad to have paid.

The black dogs pricked their ears at the sound of running feet. Needing direction, they whined and skulked around Belleme, who remained serene, apparently unconcerned by the turn of events. His stare locked with Robin's. 'Do you assume that I'm impressed by your act of cunning-man magic? Your friend had already performed the task I set him. You merely broke the connection I was about to let fall.'

Robin wasn't going to allow himself to be deviated from his path. Any exchange with the Baron was fraught with the danger of becoming entangled in his lies. Belleme served a devil, and demons served him—whatever words he used, his language was deceit. In contradiction Robin kept his next words plain, upholding the truth and strength he embodied.

'You will leave Sherwood—take your slaves with you—and never return.'

'You're banishing me from your kingdom?' Belleme gave a bark of laughter. 'But you have not yet inherited it... it is in flux until you take the place of the *old* king.' He twisted his arm in the mist, speeding up its languid curling. 'And he is weakened by the cold. It eats into his bones like worms through a corpse. I bring the heat from the realm of perpetual fire, to burn that rot away and replace it with an unending light.'

Some quality in his tone, a soothing promise of warmth, crept into the minds of all the outlaws. They had gathered beside John, trusting Robin to have the answer to their plight. Now each one of them was shivering, the touch of death spreading through their bodies with every freezing breath they inhaled. All they wanted was the comfort of a fireside, to close their eyes and rest, and forget the strictures of winter.

Robin tightened his grip on the silver arrow, held it like a wand, and allowed the cold to move through him. Grinding echoes of the ice that had carved the rock he stood upon filled his skull, wore his bones smooth, set the blood in his veins into the shapes of sleeping trees, his heart into a seed.

Made him equal to the infernal.

To Robin, the silver in his fist was the touch of snow upon a fire, the first flakes lost, but then falling thick and feathery, hissing the embers to black before encasing them in flawless white. He aimed the image at the hounds, watching with certainty as the flames in the dogs' eyes died away until they were a soft brown, white-rimmed with panic. With the heaviness and bloating of the possession lifted from them, they diminished back to the true forms of the hunting hounds they had been. Yelping and cowed from pain and confusion, they bolted for the slopes leading towards the woodland, vanishing into the fog.

The Baron de Belleme remained—a dark figure no longer given the molten lustre from the black dogs' regard, though his face was an inertly handsome ivory mask in the filtered moonlight. 'You must learn to appreciate the complexity of the powers you seek to control.' His tone was reasonable, affable even, as if offering advice to a comrade. 'Otherwise, you simply drive it ahead of you, like a herdsman goading a wild bull with a stick—it will always be awaiting its chance to turn and gore you.'

With a derisive flourish, he whisked the hem of his robes aside. Lining the silk was a coruscating shimmer, as if living flames had somehow been stitched into the fabric. 'My servants are not so easily dispensed with, *Wolfshead.*'

The outlaws reeled, arms across their faces to ward off the fierce heat. The Baron radiated contempt and dominance, outshining the silver arrow raised against him as if it were a shard of ice held before a blazing oven.

Then, an ordinary arrow hissed past Robin, then another—he span around to see Marion nocking her next shaft and aiming it at Belleme. Her expression was firm, her posture upright and head high, her hair catching the ghastly glow and turning it to beauty. She loosed again and again, every shot more fluid than the last as her thawing muscles remembered their art. Robin thrust the silver arrow into his belt and took up his own bow to join her attack. He drew out the last handful of his arrows, aimed and shot them in time with hers.

The Baron folded around the shafts as they hit, each twinned impact sending him reeling back a step, his robes closing over the flames of the jinn, so that their light was snuffed out and replaced by the night.

Will, Nasir, and Tuck hurried forward to stand with Marion, Robin, and John; spurred to overcome the torpor that numbed them, though they could still hardly lift their swords.

Much faltered, staying where he was, unable to be any closer to the Baron and the demons he sheltered—and then shook his head in horror, his caution justified, as Belleme roared with laughter and rose to his full height, spreading his cloak like phoenix wings, scattering the burnt sticks and melted blades of the arrows.

'You cannot win, Wolfshead! Your weapons,

your pathetic obstinacy, your ignorant and primitive beliefs are all fuel to the fires of my lord Azael!'

Robin passed the silver arrow to Marion. The touch of her skin scared him, it was so cold. She was beyond shivering, almost spent. There was no time to speak, but in one look, they communicated all they needed.

You are like a May morning...

Marion brought the arrow to her lips, closed her eyes, and kissed it. The heavy silver, warmed by her breath, bloomed in the dark. A gentle, green glow, as if it was under dappled sunlight, escaped between her fingers; a fledgling green, the kind that lets the sky through, turning the world to bird song and flowers. She held it to her hammering heart.

Robin saw Belleme's attention snap towards Marion and tried to deflect it back onto himself. 'You are right! We cannot fight the fires of hell. Hate burns whatever it's turned against, but it also burns the souls of those who wield it.' He could see Belleme losing interest in his homily. 'Does your soul still belong to you, *Baron?* Or are you just a slave to your devil?'

The goading worked. 'Only a peasant could mistake a loyal servant for a slave! You have no conception of how my lord Azael works through me to achieve his desires!' The flames within his robes intensified as if he stood upon a pyre. 'You will be bound by molten chains forged in hell's furnace, and your feeble god will be lured out of hiding and into my grip by your screams of agony!'

Flames curled out from the hem of Belleme's cloak, sinuous and hypnotic. He raised his arms to conduct them, his face shining in the glare. They split into three and reared above Robin's head, weaving, poised to strike.

Marion listened but did not look. Her mind teetered on the point of the silver arrow, where she could see the blunt stylised form becoming a leaf bud; the shaft roughening to a branch; the fletchings lengthening into roots. The metal growing from a weapon to a wand. She pointed it towards the Baron and opened her eyes. Holding tight to the dream-memory of when her fever broke—using that recollection, seared into her being, of deliverance.

She unfurled her fingers and released the spirit of spring.

Cool emerald light and silver petals swathed her, and for an instant she was a queen in her regalia, outshining the baleful red of the jinn. Then, the evanescence dwindled away into the seams of the rock she stood upon, splitting like lightning before it seeped into the stone.

Robin's hope was an indrawn breath of expectation—lost again when nothing changed.

His fate hung over him, dripping venom, scorching his skin, blinding him.

The hilt of a sword was pressed into his palm—instinctively he took it and felt as if Herne had gripped his hand in encouragement, but it was Much's voice by his ear. 'I kept it safe for you, Robin.'

Without thinking, he brought Albion up in an arc that sliced through the columns of flame—and as he did so, the green glow burst up from the cracks in the stone surrounding the demons, sprouting vines of light that raced up the fires, choking them with leaves and blossoms that cascaded like falling stars. Robin, his blade readied for another cut, looked to where Belleme had been standing. He saw him cowering beneath the growing light, curling in on himself like rot shrivelled by the sun. Robin forced himself forwards with Albion raised to deliver the final blow, but when he reached the Baron there was nothing left to kill—just a scattering of black ashes lost in the dazzle emanating from the earth.

He sheathed Albion.

They were enraptured.

The fog that had hemmed them in warmed to dew, sparkling on their hair and clothes, running down swords, falling like tears.

The virescent light withdrew into Marion, then through the silver arrow, and down to its fathomless winter preserve. The night mantled them—but this time it was clear; the constellations were faceted gems, and the moon setting behind the forest of Sherwood was like a shield of polished bone placed back in its armoury.

EPILOGUE

In the last darkness before the grey of dawn, a rider galloped the abandoned roads and tracks through the deepest woodland. The beat of hooves died away and was gone before it was noticed, the final faint rumbles masked by the triumphant bellowing of a stag.

Three twisting shadows followed; smoke without fire, dragged behind on leashes of sorcery.

In their stronghold, the wolves howled, sensing fleeing, weakened prey.

Safe in the womb of his cave, Herne lay back on his pallet, pulled white furs over his body and sank into sleep, his fingertips and palms stained with iron-red pigments, the blood of the earth. The guttering candle-stub at the base of the rock wall gave life to the images, and they danced and quivered in the waning light.

The flower stood straight, its thumbed chalk petals falling and snuffing out the flames painted around it, gentling them to a radiant dawn.

A hand, a hoof, a paw, an arrow, a flame, a flower…

The rising sun.

You may also enjoy…

Richard Carpenter's
ROBIN OF
SHERWOOD

OAK TREE BOOKS

THE SORCERER'S
INCANTATION

Jennifer Ash, Paul Birch,
and Paul Kane

www.ingramcontent.com/pod-product-compliance
Lightning Source LLC
Chambersburg PA
CBHW010316210626
R18465900001BA/R184659PG46814CBX00001BA/1